Day of Forgiveness

Paul Anthony

Library of Congress Control Number: 2012907310

ISBN: 978-0-9743600-2-7

https://www.Day-of-Forgiveness.com

Printed in the United States of America

Third Edition

For Mother

Table of Contents

Chapter 1: Return From the Abyss

"Another city, another hotel room," Tobias muttered as the bellhop set his suitcase on the stand at the foot of the bed. He locked the door behind him, barely glancing at the modest room before collapsing face-first onto the crisp white pillow. The book tour was wearing him down. Endless tables, endless signatures—his name scrawled across pages that felt increasingly alien, as if someone else had written the strange, controversial ideas inside.

He fielded questions from curious students and skeptical adults alike—from scientists to housewives. And though he answered patiently, he often felt just as uncertain as those who asked. His book explored predictions for the twenty-first century, casting him—somehow—as an authority on the future. It was his publisher's idea to add lectures and Q&A sessions to the tour, feeding the public's appetite for the coming New Age.

"You're selling possibilities," the publisher had said, trying to coax Tobias—who hated travel—into promoting the book. Inspired or not, the mission was grueling. He was one of many authors warning of humanity's potential demise: war, poverty, crime, climate collapse. But Tobias's work focused on tolerance and harmony with the natural world. He wrestled with how to avoid the violent end others predicted. That long road had led him here—to another hotel room, another city, and the ambiguous promise of making sense of an uncertain future.

Still in his street clothes, Tobias drifted into a restless sleep. The room darkened, and city lights glittered through the slats of the venetian blinds like scattered jewels. His phone rang. It was Mill—his agent, his friend.

"Well, did you make it there in one piece?" she asked.

"Do I sound like it?" he croaked, voice thick with sleep.

"Okay, grouchy. What's wrong?"

"This whole tour's been too much," Tobias sighed. "Yesterday in Denver, some guy told me my ideas were unfounded. Said no one could predict the future—not with math, probabilities, or logic. I told him I wasn't trying to predict anything, just offering a new lens for everyday events. He ignored the evidence and basically called me a fraud."

Mill chuckled. "He really got under your skin, huh? Since when do you bite your tongue?"

"No, Mill—this time was different. I may as well have been talking to a brick wall. Why did he even come to the lecture? Why am I putting myself through this?"

"Now, now, my dear," she soothed. "How many cities left before you're home?"

2

"Two. I can't wait to get back to New York. I hate traveling alone. If you'd been there, you probably could've handled him better."

"Oh really? Who was he?"

"Some local physics professor named Stokes. I didn't ask which school."

"Funny, Toby. They always ask about *your* credentials. You always have to prove yourself."

"You can say that again. He wasn't listening to the ideas—just grilling me about authority. He didn't want a conversation. He wanted a fight."

Mill paused. "I know the type—image over substance. But tell me, which one of you played the brick wall?"

"What?" Tobias blinked.

"We both know you can be stubborn, Toby. Maybe that's why you thought I'd handle him better. But they don't want me—they want it straight from the horse's mouth. And you're quite the horse."

Tobias exhaled, half amused. Mill always knew how to deflate his ego.

"Gee, thanks," he said dryly. "I guess you think I'm more mule than horse."

"My little pony."

"Well, in this case, the guy was just wrong."

Mill shifted gears. "Have you seen Jimmy?"

"Not yet."

"How can he be your assistant while taking college classes?"

"Come on, Mill. You know he's part-time."

"You just came from Denver alone. Is he meeting you in San Francisco? I thought he was joining you after finals."

"Yes. What time is it?"

"Nine fifteen, New York time."

"Oh, Mill—I've got to get moving. Jimmy should be here soon. I need to check out the bookstore and prep on the computer."

"No rest for the weary, huh?"

"I'll talk to you later."

"Bye."

Tobias clicked off the phone and crossed to the window behind the small oak desk. From the sixteenth floor, he looked out over downtown San Francisco. The dark sky had finally swallowed the last light of day. The city lights shimmered, beautiful but deceptive. Below, panhandlers and homeless figures moved through the streets—urban ghosts in the shadow of gleaming high-rises. The luxury hotels kept poverty at arm's length, their revolving doors spinning between two worlds: one of bellhops and conferences, the other of survival and silence.

After showering, Tobias half-listened to the television voices murmuring about political unrest, traffic delays, and weather updates—mundane concerns of the early twenty-first century. Though he made a living discussing the world of tomorrow, he knew little of the monumental events that loomed just ahead.

The hotel phone rang abruptly as he dressed, startling him. It was Jimmy.

"Hi, TS. I just got into San Francisco. I should be at the hotel in less than an hour."

"Good. I've been climbing the walls. Maybe we can kick around a few ideas."

"See you soon."

"OK."

Tobias stepped out to explore, as he often did in unfamiliar cities. He passed quietly through the carpeted hallway, past closed doors, toward the elevators. He preferred grabbing a snack from a local store over waiting for room service.

Outside, the cool breeze carried a hint of fog and sea. He inhaled deeply and walked uphill toward a busy intersection. But the crowd thinned quickly, and the buildings grew shabbier. An older man sat slumped on the sidewalk, charcoal-colored hair matted, head bowed—his age indeterminate, but his weariness unmistakable.

Tobias slowed, uneasy. He didn't want to appear lost by turning around, so he kept walking. Too late—he felt eyes on him. Raised in Philadelphia, he still had street smarts. He scanned the area, but escape routes were few. A young man was approaching fast, crossing diagonally—not like a panhandler.

"Mister, can you spare some change?"

Tobias didn't reach for his wallet. "Sorry, man."

The man's face twisted into a grim scowl. "Yeah, you're gonna be a lot sorrier. Give it up!"

His pupils were dilated, darting wildly. A dark pistol hung low in his left hand. Tobias, no fool, reached slowly for his wallet. But the man was impatient—desperate. He struck Tobias hard on the right side of his head with the gun. Tobias collapsed, his left leg jerking uncontrollably.

"Give me that wallet! Don't make me hurt you!" the mugger growled. "And the cell phone. The watch too."

He snatched everything from Tobias's pockets, sweat streaking down his face. "Get up!"

Tobias, groggy, whispered, "No."

"Get up!"

"I can't," Tobias said, his leg still twitching.

The mugger pressed the gun to Tobias's forehead. "Give me everything you got!"

"That's it. That's all," Tobias murmured.

"Well, that's it for you too!" The man pulled the trigger.

Tobias heard the click—and mercifully passed out.

He remembered little of the attack. The gun had misfired. No bullet bore his name. As he drifted in and out of consciousness in the ambulance, everything felt… different. The air. The sounds. Even the silence.

He sensed eyes on him as the stretcher lifted. *Where were all these people when I needed them?* he wondered, listening for a familiar voice in the din.

Wrapped in cool darkness, Tobias felt safe—like a cocoon shielding him from the world. Far off, a high-pitched beep echoed. Pause. Beep. Pause. Each beep grew louder. He heard movement. Low voices. *Not a cocoon*, he thought. *Or maybe a very crowded one.* He smiled faintly.

He opened his eyes. The beeping was a heart monitor. The voices belonged to doctors and nurses.

The emergency room buzzed with motion. Tobias watched them all—doctors, nurses, patients—as if they were actors on a stage. Everything looked new, strangely fascinating. Human faces seemed unfamiliar, almost alien.

A woman leaned over him.

"What's your name?" she asked.

"Tobias," he said, trying to focus.

"Last name?"

"Tobias Sinclair."

"I'm Dr. Patel," she said, pressing a cold compress to his head. Her name tag read *M. Patel, MD*. "You're in the emergency room. Do you remember anything?"

"No. What happened?"

"You were attacked. Head injury. You're lucky—it could've been worse. We'll run some tests and keep you under observation. Is there anyone we should contact?"

Tobias hesitated. Then remembered Jimmy. "Yes. My assistant should be at the Hyland Hotel. Jimmy Rudolph. I don't know his number—it's on speed dial."

"We'll call the hotel. Is he your next of kin?"

Tobias paused. "Yes… I guess he is."

"I need to ask a few questions to test your memory. Okay?"

"Okay."

"Do you remember what happened?"

"I left the hotel for a walk. A guy asked for money. Next thing I know, I'm here."

"Do you know where you are?"

"Looks like a hospital to me, Doc."

Dr. Patel smiled. "What city?"

"Denver."

"Denver?"

"I've been traveling a lot." Tobias blinked. "This is San Francisco, isn't it?"

"Yes. Are you in pain?"

"Just a headache. Right here." He rubbed his temple. "It won't go away."

"Headaches are common after head trauma. I'll prescribe something."

Tobias hesitated. "Doctor… something feels different. You'll think I'm crazy, but…"

"Yes?"

"Everything around me looks… off. I know I'm in a hospital. I know who I am. But everything—the building, the stretchers, the people—it all seems crude. Primitive."

"Primitive? Even the computers?"

"Maybe *rudimentary* is better. But here's the strangest part: even people seem rudimentary. You and me included. Like lost animals. Like we don't know our true reality."

Dr. Patel blinked. "You've lost me, Mr. Sinclair."

"I don't understand it either," Tobias said, "but since waking up, I've been trying to answer your questions while ignoring this strange feeling—like everything around me is undeveloped. Backward."

Dr. Patel nodded gently. "It's common to feel disoriented after head trauma. Let's see how you feel in the morning."

Tobias felt dismissed but said nothing. After the final round of questions, scans, and sutures, Dr. Patel admitted him for observation. The police came to interview him, but he couldn't recall enough to be helpful. They left quickly.

Finally able to rest, Tobias surrendered to the care of nurses and staff—strangers sworn to preserve his well-being. He, who rarely let anyone care for him, now relented. *Angels of mercy,* he thought as he drifted into sleep.

He had barely slipped into slumber when Jimmy arrived, whispering softly.

"TS? Are you asleep?"

Tobias, groggy from medication, mumbled, "Sleep? What's that?" He turned his head and offered a crooked smile.

Jimmy stood near the door, beside the empty second bed—its bare mattress folded like a forgotten promise. He exhaled, relieved. He'd searched frantically after Tobias failed to answer his phone. A hotel employee had mentioned an ambulance. Jimmy had checked the wrong hospital first.

"It's good to see a familiar face," Tobias said, forcing himself awake. "How long have you been here?"

"I got to the hotel just after they took you. I've been all over town looking."

"I can be slippery when I want to be." Tobias chuckled, then winced.

"Are you feeling okay?"

"I'm alright. They're keeping me for observation. Gave me a sleeping pill. Did you talk to the bookstore?"

"I called on the way here. They postponed the signing. Said you can reschedule anytime." Jimmy shook his head. "TS, you're always thinking about work."

Tobias yawned. "Jimmy, something's going on in my head—and it's not just the headache."

"The doctor said you had a seizure."

"That's what they said. But I don't remember much. That guy hit me hard. Still, this is something else." Tobias hesitated. "I hope you don't think I'm losing it when I tell you…"

"Tell me what?"

"That I feel… a strange compulsion."

"A compulsion?"

"Let me finish," Tobias said gently. "Since waking up, I've wanted to tell everyone that they're wrong. About everything."

"Wrong? About how to run a hospital?"

"No, Jimmy. I mean wrong about what we believe we are."

Jimmy blinked. "What do we believe we are?"

Tobias paused. Jimmy looked up to him, and Tobias didn't want to lose that trust. He had to go slowly.

"I know it sounds strange, but I see people differently now. I don't think I'm crazy. I just think everyone should see what I see."

"What do you see?" Jimmy asked, genuinely curious.

Tobias's eyes glistened. He fought the sleepiness and tried to be understood. "What if our creation, development, and history aren't what we thought? What if we're meant to set a new standard of knowledge and self-understanding?"

Jimmy smiled. "C'mon, TS. Isn't that what your books are about? The New Age?"

"Yes, but this feels different. I don't just write about it—I feel like I'm part of it. Like I'm supposed to shape it."

"What?" Jimmy teased. "You mean you've got a calling to be a preacher?"

"No, not religious. It's more like… if I don't share this, we'll all suffer. I'm serious, Jimmy. Everything looks different—even you. The world feels different. I can't explain it. But I know one thing: that blow to my head did something. I think I have knowledge people need."

Tobias yawned again. "Sleeping pill's kicking in."

"Get some rest. I'll be here first thing in the morning."

Tobias was already drifting off. Jimmy watched him sleep, head bandaged, body still. Guilt and shame welled up.

"If I'd been there," Jimmy whispered, "no one would've dared touch you."

He studied Tobias's profile, distorted slightly by the pillow. He sat beside the bed, thinking of what could've happened—what almost did. And what might never have happened if Tobias hadn't hired him when no one else would.

Jimmy stood, dimmed the light, and returned to the hotel to rest.

—

Before dawn, Tobias dreamed of the gun again.

"No! It's going to hurt," he cried aloud.

He awoke with the same headache. Everything hurt— his body, his head, the light, the noise, the television, the clatter of the hospital floor.

An older nurse entered with medication.

"What's going to hurt?" she asked.

Tobias looked up. "I thought the gun..." He looked away. "Never mind."

The nurse, heavyset with a Caribbean accent, smiled warmly as she prepared to take his blood pressure.

"Good morning, Mr. Sinclair. I'm Carmen. I'll be your nurse today. How are you feeling?"

"Like I got hit by a train. My head's pounding."

"Did you sleep?"

"Not much. Bad dreams."

"Nightmares? Flashbacks?"

Tobias frowned. "Yes. Bits and pieces of the mugging. It's coming back—like reruns in my head. I always wake up before the hit."

Carmen wrapped the cuff around his arm. "Sometimes being threatened is worse than being hit."

Tobias yawned.

"You get some rest now. Breakfast will be here soon— it's still early." She dimmed the blinds. "When they catch that thief, they should lock him up and throw away the key."

Soft morning light filtered in. Tobias stared at the off-white ceiling, listening to the ticking clock. Outside his door, the hospital stirred to life.

As the medication took hold, his thoughts drifted to the street below. To the young man who had robbed him. To the long road that had led him here.

He mentally retraced the past few years. After his second book sold modestly, he needed income. Mill and his publisher pushed him onto the lecture circuit. He traveled constantly, sharing New Age insights with curious audiences.

Now, the effort felt overwhelming. The tour had landed him in a hospital. And the knowledge he once embraced now frightened him.

He could see things others couldn't—but that clarity came with fear. Entering new territory always scared him, even as he sought it. That contradiction had led him into danger.

Predicting the future still felt unfamiliar. He didn't fear rejection for claiming elusive knowledge. What he feared was the isolation it might bring.

Later that morning, Tobias ate breakfast in bed, propped up on two pillows. He felt strangely alert—aware of every detail in the room. "I must tell them the truth," he murmured, chewing toast and jam, only half understanding what he meant. Something in him felt spiritually reinvigorated.

Carmen, the nurse from earlier, entered with his medication.

"Good morning, Mr. Sinclair. I'm working a double shift today, so you're stuck with me a bit longer." She smiled. "Oh, I see you're smiling. Does that mean you don't need this pain medication?"

"Now that you mention it, the headache's gone. I'm feeling better."

The television was on, reporting a suicide bombing in the Middle East.

Carmen sucked her teeth. "Look at that. All this senseless killing. Want me to change the channel?"

"Yes, thank you. Loud noises still bother me." He paused, watching the carnage. "How can people do that to each other? Killing is bad enough—but indiscriminate murder with bombs…"

Thinking he was still traumatized, Carmen switched the channel. A televangelist now preached to a congregation of mostly older people, promising health, wealth, love, and happiness. Dressed in fine clothes, the minister looked into the camera and nearly wept. *"You should receive the blessing of abundance. The Lord does not want you to be poor."*

Carmen glanced at Tobias. "I read one of your books, Mr. Sinclair."

Tobias sat up. "Oh? So my nurse is a fan, I hope."

"I enjoyed it. If I may ask—doesn't your book say the same thing this preacher is saying? That everyone should get their piece of the pie?"

"Well, Carmen, I think the pie should be big enough for all of us to enjoy."

"I liked how you said the New Age should be for everyone."

"Maybe so," Tobias replied, cautious. "But that's not quite what I meant."

"What did you mean?"

"I meant people shouldn't fight over resources. Just being human should entitle everyone to a decent quality of life—good buildings, roads, sewers—no matter where they live."

"No differences?"

"That's right. I wrote that everyone's standard of living should be similar—whether in Africa, Asia, Australia, Europe, North or South America."

"That would be nice. But is it realistic?"

"I think the only reason we have such dramatic differences is because we cling to artificial divisions—countries, ethnic groups, races, religions. We fight over limited resources. And when I talk about wealth distribution, people accuse me of socialism or communism."

"So you're saying the haves should have—and the have-nots should have too?"

"Ideally, there should be no haves or have-nots." Tobias saw Carmen was intrigued, but he wanted to avoid a political debate. He sighed. "I'm just saying every person is of equal value. Everyone deserves a reasonably equal standard of living."

"No rich or poor?"

"There should be a minimal universal standard—a baseline of comfort and dignity. I have to admit, I was following the herd, writing New Age books with the same language and philosophy as everyone else. I forgot that most of the world goes to bed hungry."

Carmen tried to shift the mood. "I guess the only answer to poverty is to completely change the world."

Tobias looked up at the televangelist, who promised heaven on earth. Something in him resisted. He'd never been religious—not since his adolescent disillusionment. But now, a strange spiritual fire stirred within.

He stared at the screen and nearly shouted, "This preacher is saying God gives more to those who already have too much—and calls it a blessing of abundance. We already have more abundance in this country than three-quarters of the world! He's not talking about how hard it is for a rich man to enter the kingdom of heaven."

Carmen stared. Tobias realized he'd said too much.

Against her better judgment, she replied, "It is easier for a camel to go through the eye of a needle..."

"I see you know Scripture," Tobias said, regaining composure.

"Not as well as I'd like. But I try to study the Word. Are you sure you're not a preacher yourself, Mr. Sinclair?" Carmen smiled, half curious, half puzzled. She remembered the cardinal rule: don't discuss politics or religion with patients—a rule she often broke.

Dr. Patel entered. "Good morning, Mr. Sinclair."

Carmen shared the vital signs and made a quick exit.

"You look much better," Dr. Patel said. "How are you feeling?"

"Better. Not brand new, but close. The headache's gone."

"Good. Any further seizures, sleep issues, unusual thoughts?"

Tobias hesitated. He didn't want to mention the nightmare—or the thoughts swirling in his head. He feared being labeled psychotic.

"No, I feel fine," he said, more out of fear than truth. He worried Carmen might tell the doctor about his outburst. "Just a little jumpy," he muttered to himself, wondering if his caution was the first sign of paranoia.

Dr. Patel nodded. "All your tests look good. You can be discharged tomorrow. Will someone be here to accompany you?"

"Yes. My assistant will be here."

"The nurse will go over discharge instructions. Take it easy."

"You too, Doc. Take it easy," Tobias said, eyes gleaming—using humor to shield himself.

Dr. Patel didn't smile. "I meant you should take things slowly. Avoid too much activity. And come back if anything feels off."

"Thanks, Doc."

Tobias waited for Jimmy to return. He needed to share what he thought he knew—before the thoughts consumed him. He was puzzled, uncertain. He'd always been enthusiastic about sharing his New Age ideas, but he'd never wanted to be a zealot.

This time felt different.

He didn't want to repeat the mistake of his first book—telling everyone everything. He'd been labeled eccentric, even a kook. Lost his job. But he'd turned lemons into lemonade, embracing his eccentricities and writing about them.

He didn't have much of a reputation to protect. But he wanted to be taken seriously. And he knew he had to be careful.

Four years ago, Tobias moved from Philadelphia to New York after losing his job as an attorney for a nonprofit legal group. "We're downsizing," his supervisor had said, as if that softened the blow.

He was let go shortly after releasing his first book—an irreverent tome criticizing the government and proposing a new legal structure based on universal principles. At work, he was seen as a radical nonconformist who jeopardized their government funding.

He had to go.

The book gained modest popularity. Tobias knew he needed change. New York was similar to Philly, but still required adjustment. He suspected the real reason for his dismissal wasn't economics—it was the book, written under a barely disguised pen name.

He was a victim of his own modest success.

"Law is my living, but it's not my life," he'd say. He remained a proud nonconformist—always drawn to the unusual.

Throughout his childhood, Tobias had always been unconventional—different from the rest of his family. His father, Willie, a postal worker with a tough exterior that melted in the presence of his children, sacrificed his dream of becoming a jazz musician for the security of a steady job. He wanted Tobias, Janice, and Little Willie—his firstborn and namesake—to have a stable childhood and a better future.

Big Willie partnered with his younger brother, Uncle Kevin, a construction laborer, to buy a three-family house. The idea came from Tobias's mother, Rebecca—a petite, graceful woman who seemed too delicate to manage two households, yet somehow did. After Tobias was born, she grew tired of commuting to distant suburbs and returned to school to study nursing. Even after graduating, she remained a quiet force—guiding her family as an equal partner to Big Willie.

Her subtle advice often inspired him. "We'll have room for us and for Kevin's family," she proposed. "And the third apartment will help us through thin times. You know Kevin's work is seasonal, and you can't carry the whole family alone."

"I've only got one brother," Willie would grumble in defense of Kevin. Rebecca knew when to pull back and let him reflect. She and her sister-in-law, Gladys, gently persuaded the brothers to take control of their destiny.

After the purchase, Rebecca convinced Willie to rent the third apartment to her aging mother. "It's steady income from her pension, and we can keep an eye on her."

So Tobias grew up in a house filled with family: his uncle, aunt, and cousins on the floor below; his grandmother above; and his own family sandwiched in the middle.

As the youngest, Tobias grew quickly. His family often retold the story of how, at age three, he saved them from a fire. One chilly Friday evening, his father came home with coworkers to play cards and drink beer. No one noticed the closet—until Tobias, standing near the stairway, pointed and exclaimed, "Ooooh, look at the fire!"

A lit cigarette had ignited an overcoat. At first, his father smiled—then saw the flames. He and the others rushed to extinguish the fire while Rebecca scooped Tobias into her arms and carried him outside, followed by Janice and Little Willie.

That moment became legend. It marked Tobias as someone who saw what others missed—and planted in him a quiet need to protect those he loved.

In first and second grade, Tobias was bussed out of his neighborhood to a predominantly White school as part of racial integration. He adapted well at first, singing "We Shall Overcome" and "If I Had a Hammer" in music class, reciting poems about brotherhood, and dreaming of a color-blind society.

But on the playground and in the cafeteria, he was met with silence. He thought he'd done something wrong, unaware that the color of his skin was the reason. The parents of those children had already taught them to avoid little Black boys. It was the mid-1960s—there were no images of children like Tobias on television or in popular culture.

By third grade, most of the White families had moved away, and the school became predominantly Black. It made little sense to travel so far for a school that mirrored the one around the corner. Tobias returned to his neighborhood school—but now he was seen as an outsider.

It soon became clear he was different—especially in math. By fifth grade, he could work with numbers in the millions while classmates struggled with thousands. Whether this gift was innate or shaped by his earlier schooling was unclear. But it earned him admiration. Neighborhood kids came to him for homework help.

Tobias didn't chase popularity or sports. He saw the world differently. He embraced his isolation, becoming a quirky loner. Other children teased him for being different, for his unusual interests. He was the brains of the group—but not the leader. He lacked athletic grace and grew shy, retreating into books and projects.

In adolescence, he grew tired of the "nerd" label and tried to fit in—sometimes pretending not to understand things. But that only made him seem condescending. Eventually, he chose to be himself, warts and all. He realized others would accept him more easily if he accepted himself.

Gradually, he found a clique of bookworm teens. It wasn't the worst fate in high school—and far better than childhood isolation. Within this group, they debated the world in splendid isolation, turning their ostracism into a snobbish asset. It was in this circle that Tobias met Sharon—his high school sweetheart, future wife, and mother of his son.

Though he excelled academically, his path to law school wasn't direct. He considered physics, astronomy, engineering, and mathematics. But he eventually chose law—hoping to serve those who couldn't help themselves. He wanted to put out the fires of injustice.

As an attorney, Tobias gave voice to the voiceless— navigating red tape and discrimination. But he felt stifled by a system built to oppress through complexity and conformity. He was a small fish in a vast, indifferent ocean.

Outside of work, he shared his intellectual and scientific interests with anyone who would listen—friends, coworkers, neighbors. He turned to writing. But soon, his writings and his job collided.

At work, they whispered, "There's that weird lawyer who wrote that book."

"How can people believe you now?" his supervisor asked before letting him go.

"Had you even considered your career?" a coworker asked.

"No," Tobias replied. "This was too important to sacrifice. It felt like a calling—something higher."

He had no regrets, though the cost was steep.

After losing his job, Tobias faced a choice: hot or cold, salty or sweet, lawyer or writer. He asked Mill—his friend since law school—what she thought.

"The answer's clear," she said. "Do what you love."

Tobias's niche became clear: exploring the relevance of the New Age for poor communities and people of color. Yet the attendees at New Age conventions were worlds apart from the clients he once served as an attorney. He missed those people more than he missed the law itself.

He had always wanted to connect with those in need— across backgrounds and ethnicities. His writing career had its rewards, but the conventions often drew only the affluent, and few attendees looked like him. Still, his book signings and lectures began attracting more young people and more people of color than was typical for a New Age author. They saw themselves in Tobias—not just as an African American, but as someone still young enough to speak their language. He had just turned forty.

Many came with a question: *Is there a place for us in the future?*

"I guess I'm the Lieutenant Uhura of New Age writers," Tobias would quip.

He tapped into their need. His second book, *The New Age for All People*, examined how societal change might affect people of color in both industrialized and developing nations. It struck a nerve. Few New Age writers had addressed the future of those with limited resources.

One reviewer wrote:

In his first book, Tobias Sinclair presented a plausible explanation of how the universe works. Now, in his second, he asks whether the New Age is truly for all people. Can we share the world equally and peacefully, living as a united species without disparity? Sinclair poses challenging, provocative questions—none of them easy to answer.

The attention bolstered Tobias's resolve. As an African American, he knew he had a unique lens on the New Age story. It became not just a calling, but a way to make a living. His heart was no longer in law. He needed change— and New York, with its people and publishers, felt right. Mill was there, too.

Unlike other writers chasing trends, Tobias felt he was teaching truth. His intentions were pure. He was once again that three-year-old boy warning of fire—urging others to step off the tracks before the train arrived.

So he packed his things, loaded a rental car, and drove to New York to take a long shot at a new life.

—

In New York, Tobias stayed close to Mill—a native with a blunt sense of humor he secretly admired. He found an apartment near her home in Park Slope and lived off savings, writing and bouncing ideas off Mill over coffee and pastries.

"Toby," she teased after his second book launched, "either they'll think you're nuts, or they'll say you're a genius. I'm still trying to figure out which."

"That makes two of us," he replied.

Mill eventually pursued entertainment law, but she was a Jill-of-all-trades—part agent, part manager, part performer. Outgoing, adventurous, and lively, she was the opposite of the subdued Tobias.

They met in law school. Mill had noticed Tobias sitting alone in the back of the lecture hall, avoiding contact. Neither remembered who asked for that first cup of coffee, but they became fast friends and study partners.

Mill was older than most students, with a brief corporate career behind her. She had escaped a bad marriage—an abusive husband who resented her ambition. With few biological relatives, Mill once told Tobias, "All people are cousins. I suppose the whole world is my family."

Her lack of family made her vulnerable to the man she thought she loved. But she found the courage to leave him—no children, no regrets.

Ironically, her divorce fueled her drive to study law. Accepted to only one school, she clung to the opportunity like a life preserver. She sat in the back of the lecture hall, a loner like Tobias, wearing her badge of courage openly.

By then, Tobias had drifted from his wife, Sharon, who raised their son alone while he pursued college and law school. The marriage faded, eclipsed by his intellectual pursuits.

Neither Tobias nor Mill mourned their failed marriages. They saw law school as salvation—from the world, and for the world. A quiet, awkward Black man and a bold, outspoken White woman—they complemented each other. Their friendship remained platonic, like siblings in a playful rivalry. They stayed close after graduation, despite choosing vastly different legal paths.

Over the years, both grew disillusioned with the profession. Mill remained a frustrated performer, haunted by her past. Tobias wrestled with being an idealist born too late—unable to find rose-colored glasses.

"What a pair we make," Mill would say. "You and I need to make decisions. Either do it or get off the pot!"

Tobias grew to love Mill—and New York—for their no-nonsense, shoot-straight style. It energized him.

—

Now, in a hospital bed in San Francisco, Tobias reflected. Had he made the right choice—leaving law for a dream, a compulsion, a quirky vision and a nonconformist friend?

Was it worth getting his head bashed in, lying beneath fluorescent lights in a far-off city?

Should he have stayed on the traditional path—career, wife, family?

He tried to block thoughts of his failed marriage. Of the son he'd left behind in Philadelphia. The young man he barely knew.

He drifted into a restless sleep, waiting for Jimmy to arrive.

—

Jimmy, meanwhile, woke late—exhausted from the chaos of the past day. He'd gotten a room just down the hall from Tobias's, knowing Tobias would likely be discharged soon.

Tobias would still want to attend the book signing before flying back to New York. He was pragmatic like that.

Jimmy could almost hear him say, "Well, we came all this way. May as well get the job done."

Jimmy glanced at the clock—almost a quarter past eight. He had to hurry. Tobias would want to return to the hotel after discharge. To save time, Jimmy ordered breakfast through room service.

Just months ago, he never imagined working for Tobias, let alone staying in a high-rise hotel in California, ordering room service. Less than a year ago, he was nearly homeless—crashing at Yolanda's apartment when not working at the bookstore. Yolanda was his girlfriend. A baby was on the way.

Jimmy was twenty-three, born and raised in East Harlem. His father, a bear of a man from Virginia, was in jail. His mother, who came to New York from Puerto Rico as a child, was lost to addiction. Their neighborhood hadn't yet been touched by gentrification—it was still tough, still raw.

His grandmother, who spoke only Spanish, raised him. From his earliest memories, Jimmy served as her interpreter. He adored her. They protected each other from the world. She kept his life stable—always a warm plate waiting when he came home from school.

Until the day he returned to a cold stove and found her slumped at the kitchen table, head down, as if asleep.

From that moment, Jimmy was on his own. He grew up fast. Navigated foster homes and group homes until he turned eighteen. He taught himself to fight, to survive. He became a chameleon—reflecting whatever the moment required. He could play basketball in the hood by day and attend a poetry reading in the East Village by night. He could hang with Harlem street kids or downtown rockers. He could party with the best of them.

It was at one of those parties that he met Yolanda. They connected instantly—both in their final year of foster care, both functioning as emancipated minors. Though tempted by fast money, Jimmy chose work. He walked a tightrope—maintaining street credibility while taking evening classes at City College, perched like a castle above the Harlem tenements.

"I've come too far to let the streets take me down now," he told Yolanda.

Eventually, he landed an inventory job at a bookstore in Lower Manhattan—thanks to a downtown friend. The shop was barely solvent, cluttered with rare and out-of-print books. But it opened a new world to Jimmy—a world where science and spirituality intertwined. He sensed that

30

the answers he'd been chasing might be hidden in those shelves.

Ten months earlier, he'd read Tobias's second book. It described a future where people of all backgrounds shared a new vision of humanity. When Jimmy learned Tobias would be speaking at the store, he knew it wasn't coincidence.

He swapped shifts to be there. During the lecture, he was captivated by Tobias's ease, his clarity. Afterward, Jimmy approached him—awkward, towering, clutching his worn copy of the book.

"I read your book," he whispered. "I want to learn more."

Tobias looked up. "I'm glad it inspired you. What would you like to learn?"

"I want to know how it all fits together. What my place is in the world."

Tobias studied him—saw the innocence behind the guarded eyes. "No book can teach you all that. But there are guideposts. Things a young man like you can use to navigate."

"Guideposts?"

"Not quite rules. But ways to live with purpose. To seek enlightenment."

"But your book goes further," Jimmy said. "I think it applies to individual lives as well as society."

Tobias, impressed, asked, "What's your name?"

Startled, Jimmy replied, "Jimmy."

Tobias signed the book: *To Jimmy: Always learn more. Tobias Sinclair.*

Then he looked up. "Meet me after the signing."

When the last book was signed, Tobias motioned to Jimmy, still lingering in the back. "Let's grab a cup of coffee," he said with a shy grin.

They stepped into the damp night. The rain had cleared, leaving the asphalt glistening under amber streetlights.

"I know a little place down the street," Jimmy offered, recalling a diner nearby.

They walked side by side. Tobias studied him.

"Jimmy, it's good to see someone like you at my lecture. I don't usually get many guys in their twenties."

"I'm twenty-three. I guess it takes time to try to understand the world."

"Exactly. You're an exception."

"Well, I cheated. I work at that bookstore."

"That's a good thing—working and keeping an open mind. You can't beat that."

"Thanks, Mr. Sinclair."

"Call me Tobias."

"Okay," Jimmy said, though he'd always feel more comfortable calling him TS—a quiet sign of respect.

They entered the well-lit diner and slid into a booth halfway down the aisle.

"You said you wanted to learn more," Tobias said as the waitress left with their order.

"Yeah. I think I get the gist of your writing—that humanity's headed for a big change. That we can avoid war and violence by living in harmony with nature and each other. And I see what you're doing—showing how people of color and the developing world fit into the New Age."

"It sounds like you've already learned a lot, Jimmy. I want to reach as many young people as I can—people from all backgrounds. Maybe you can help me understand how to reach them. What do your friends think about the New Age?"

"Nothing much," Jimmy said. "Most of my friends don't want to know about it. Some like the idea of nature and vegetarianism. Others think it's a crock. They're more into music, clothes, cars, and bling. That stuff never impressed me. Your books talk about a different world— one I might actually belong to."

"Sounds like you find today's world hard to take."

"I've had a few knocks. But I'm taking classes at City College now."

"You're on the right path, Jimmy. Education makes it easier to understand the principles of the New Age."

"Things like spirit and faith feel more real to me than clothes and cars," Jimmy said, lighting up. "That's what I meant when I said I want to learn more. I want to understand this world—and my place in it."

"That's the million-dollar question," Tobias smiled. "What are you studying?"

"Chemistry and education. I'll be a science teacher next year."

Tobias's face brightened. "We need people with scientific knowledge—and we always need teachers. That's the key to understanding the New Age." He grew more serious. "I need an assistant. Someone with an eye for detail, but also someone who sees the absurdity of it all— with a little sense of humor."

"Sounds like a good job," Jimmy said, unsure.

"Think it over for a few days. My gut says you might be the right person—if you're interested."

They talked past midnight. That night, Jimmy became Tobias's part-time assistant. Now, ten months later, riding in a San Francisco taxi to pick up his boss, Jimmy felt he was more than an assistant. He hadn't outgrown the job— he'd grown into it.

—

At the hospital, Tobias was dressed and seated near the window, gazing at the hills and houses. Jimmy bounced into the room.

"Hey, TS! Ready to roll?"

"Ready to roll, rock, and do backflips. I've been discharged, and I'm itching to get out of here. I want a real lunch."

Outside, Tobias said, "Let's walk. There must be a good place nearby."

"I saw a little restaurant a few blocks up," Jimmy said, nodding toward the busy street.

As they walked, Jimmy asked, "Now tell me how you're really feeling, TS."

"I'm okay, I guess. But some strange things have been happening."

"Like what?"

"When I see people, they look the same—but I see them differently. Like strange animals, unaware of their surroundings."

"You mean like *Planet of the Apes*?"

"No, Jimmy. People still look like people. But it's like I know something they don't. Like everyone's blind—and I'm the only one who can see." Tobias paused. "And something else—I couldn't stop talking, almost debating, with my nurse. About religion, race… things I don't usually talk about."

"So what else is new, TS?"

"No, Jimmy. I'm serious."

They climbed the steep hill. Jimmy was surprised. Tobias usually handled questions with gentle explanations and quiet objectivity. Arguing over religion wasn't like him.

"You? Mr. Peace and Love had a disagreement with a nurse? How did that happen?"

"I don't know. I'm human, I guess. I got extremely annoyed with her views—more than I've felt in a long time."

"Are you sure you're okay?"

"Yes—but stop asking me that," Tobias snapped. "I've got all kinds of thoughts swirling in my head."

"What kinds of thoughts?"

"I keep thinking how important it is for the world to be better informed. So people can live in peace. So we can..." Tobias paused.

"So we can what?"

"So we can be a successful species. I keep thinking we'll all die—or our society will—if we don't restructure how we see ourselves."

"What do you mean?"

36

"To be honest, Jimmy, I don't even know. But these thoughts—they're different from the New Age philosophies I wrote about."

"You know, TS, this doesn't sound like you. I've never heard you talk like this. Are you sure you're okay?"

"There you go again," Tobias said, exasperated.

"Listen, TS. You've got one more lecture. Want me to cancel it? We could head back to New York and call it a day."

"I'm tired. But let's do the signing and then go home. It'll be my swan song before we shift gears. I didn't mean to make you nervous. I've just got a lot of thoughts jockeying for position in my brain. By the way—when are we going to the bookstore?"

"I knew you'd ask. I called them this morning. They said you can do it whenever you'd like."

"Let's do it tomorrow. Then fly home right after."

Jimmy smiled. "Why waste a good trip?"

"You've read my mind."

"That's not hard, TS. You're pretty predictable," Jimmy said, holding the diner door open.

They sat at a booth near the front window, discussing plans for the next day and the flight home.

"You're my right-hand man," Tobias said. He thought of his son, David—just a few years younger than Jimmy,

37

living with Tobias's mother in Philadelphia. Tobias stared past Jimmy, wondering what David was doing now.

His ex-wife, Sharon, had died in a car accident. Tobias realized that even if he'd stayed with her, his fate would be the same: he was alone.

"Doesn't this place remind you of that diner in the Village after your first book signing?" Jimmy asked.

"Yes. It sure does," Tobias said, returning to the moment. "That's when you became my right-hand man."

"Too bad you're left-handed," Jimmy said, and they both laughed.

Then silence.

Jimmy worried Tobias was still showing signs of head trauma. Tobias feared the injury had unlocked a Pandora's box of knowledge—perhaps best left untouched.

One youthful and enthusiastic. The other seasoned and serious. They finished their meal and took a cab past the bookstore so Tobias could see the location. Then they returned to the hotel and turned in early, resting for the day ahead.

Chapter 2: We Are One

The next morning, Tobias was awakened by the telephone in his hotel room. It was Jimmy.

"Are you still asleep?"

"No," said Tobias. "I just like to look at the insides of my eyelids."

"You're a funny guy."

"What time is it?"

"Nine thirty."

"When are we due at the bookstore?"

"At noon; we'll catch the lunch crowd at the bookstore. There will also be local press there. I booked us on a flight leaving for New York around four thirty. We should be home by tonight."

"Good thinking, Jimmy. I'd better get started. Meet me here in about a half hour. I'll order breakfast, and we can check out around eleven. What do you want?"

"Scrambled eggs and toast. And orange juice, too."

"You got it."

Jimmy arrived at Tobias's room just as room service was leaving. The tray was placed on the large round table at the far end of the room. Jimmy sat down at the table while

Tobias tied his tie. Tobias looked at Jimmy in the mirror's reflection.

"Don't mind me; just dig in," said Tobias, never one for formalities. He continued, "Jimmy, how did you arrange everything so fast? And what did you say about the local press?"

"Oh, it wasn't so hard. This bookstore is always busier at lunchtime. All I had to do was let the local newspapers and college press know about the change in timing." Jimmy paused. "You know, there is a lot more interest in you and your books since you were in the hospital."

"Everyone knew about the mugging?"

"It wasn't front-page news, but there may have been a line or two."

"Great." Tobias sighed.

Tobias and Jimmy finished their breakfast and took a cab to the bookstore, arriving twenty-five minutes early. The store buzzed with quiet anticipation. A mix of curious passersby and intentional attendees filled the space, drawn in by the sign in the window:

TOBIAS SINCLAIR APPEARING TODAY AT NOON.

The crowd was mostly couples and singles in their thirties and forties, many clutching copies of Tobias's latest book. Some were eager for autographs, others for answers. In the back room, Tobias spoke briefly with the bookstore owner while Jimmy lingered near the entrance, listening to fragments of conversation.

41

The attendees expected a lecture on the New Age and a discussion on self-empowerment. But Jimmy sensed something deeper stirring in Tobias. Ever since the hospital, Tobias had changed. His words carried a weight Jimmy couldn't quite name. He didn't know what Tobias would say—but he knew it wouldn't be what the crowd expected.

After a short introduction, Tobias entered the main room and approached the podium. His eyes scanned the crowd, calm but intense. The room fell silent.

"Forget all that you have been taught," Tobias began. "Or at least, question your present way of thinking—about our species, our planet, and our universe."

He paused, letting the words settle.

"We are embarking on an adventure. One of history and prehistory. One within ourselves. And one that may shape our future. Humanity is on the verge of a new understanding—of who we truly are and where we might go. What a wonderful thing it is to be human. We may even begin to understand the concept of God."

A few murmurs rippled through the crowd.

"We need to shift the way we view our world. We are one of many species that evolved on this planet. That's all. But what a magnificent species we can be."

Tobias spoke of human evolution—not just biological, but emotional and spiritual. He described how our inability to see beyond the physical world had limited us. Those who claimed to perceive more were often dismissed as mystics, psychics, or mad.

42

"If we focus only on the material," he said, "we will never overcome our violent and competitive nature. We have the potential to be great—but we sabotage it every time."

A woman near the front raised an eyebrow. "Every time?"

"Yes. I believe humanity has been through all this before," Tobias replied, his voice steady.

"You seem so certain," she said.

"Like miners trapped in a collapsed shaft, we are still buried beneath the rubble of our last global civilization. But there is light. A new way of seeing—one that may bring us back. If we embrace it, perhaps this time we won't destroy ourselves."

"What kind of light?"

"Ancient knowledge. Forgotten science. Look at Machu Picchu, the Sphinx, Puma Punku—structures built with precision we still struggle to explain. These remnants suggest a level of understanding we've lost. If we rediscover it, we may evolve—not just technologically, but spiritually."

"But how do we evolve spiritually? What does that even mean?"

"It means choosing love over division. Seeing ourselves as one species. It sounds simple, doesn't it? But we've failed at this again and again."

43

"What kinds of divisions?"

"Country. Race. Religion. Money."

"But aren't those things real?"

Tobias paused.

"They're real only to the extent that we make them real. Real by consensus. Real by the value we assign. Money is paper. Borders are lines on a map. Race is pigment shaped by sunlight and time."

A young woman raised her hand. "Are you saying race isn't real? Even though we can see the differences?"

"We see differences, yes. But we choose to make them matter. The truth is simpler, and more beautiful: we are all variations of the same design. Our skin tones are echoes of the landscapes we've walked—shaped by sun, sand, forest, and ice. We are long-lost siblings molded by the earth itself."

A teenage boy chimed in, "Like polar bears and grizzlies—they're all bears!"

Tobias smiled. "Exactly. And we're all human. The tragedy is that we've forgotten. We've mistaken adaptation for separation. We've let language, culture, and appearance convince us that we are strangers. But we are not. We are one."

An older woman raised her hand. "Pardon me, but I still don't see what this has to do with the New Age and the future of humankind."

Tobias stepped forward, his voice steady.

"Our inability to see past these divisions is the flaw that keeps repeating. It's why civilizations rise and fall. Atlantis, Lemuria, the Mayans—they all speak of cycles. Of brilliance lost to arrogance. Of unity shattered by fear."

At that moment, Claire Jenkins, a local reporter, stood up with a microphone. A cameraman hovered behind her, recording.

"Mr. Sinclair," she asked, "what specifically do you think is this flaw in humanity? And how can we overcome it?"

Tobias looked directly at her.

"The flaw is in our evolution—but not just biological. It's emotional. Spiritual. We've adapted to survive, but not to love. We've built tools, but not trust."

He paused, then continued.

"Some scientists believe we were once shaped by the sea. That our breath, our brains, even our speech may have emerged from a time when we lived at the water's edge. If true, it means we've always been adapting. Always evolving. But now, we must evolve by choice—not just by necessity."

Claire leaned in. "What kind of evolution do you mean?"

Tobias's gaze swept the room.

"An evolution of awareness. Of empathy. Of unity. We must choose to see ourselves as one species. Not divided by borders or beliefs, but united by breath and being. That is the New Age. Not crystals or chants—but consciousness. A shift in how we see ourselves, and each other."

Tobias took a breath, surprised by how easily the answers came.

"We humans are too smart for our own good," he said. "We carry the violent impulses of our primate past—aggression, fear, the need for hierarchy. And now we wield advanced technology with those same instincts. We build with brilliance, but act with brutality."

Claire nodded, absorbing the shift in tone.

"Our intelligence outpaced our wisdom," Tobias continued. "We became as clever as dolphins, as dexterous as chimpanzees, and as aggressive as wolves. We became our own worst enemy."

He paused, then added quietly, "We often speak of a doomsday or an Antichrist. But we don't need a separate destroyer. We need only look in the mirror. The flaw is in us."

The room fell silent. Claire remained focused, her voice steady.

"From your recent books, Mr. Sinclair, I understand that you're predicting the end of the world. And there's even a specific date," she said with mock astonishment. The audience leaned in, now witnesses to something larger than a book signing.

"I'm not predicting anything," Tobias replied. "I'm commenting on the evidence. And the evidence suggests a major shift for humankind in the early twenty-first century. It's more than just the Mayan calendar ending."

"What other kind of evidence?"

Tobias relaxed slightly, sensing Claire's genuine interest.

"Fragments from our past. Echoes of our future. You've heard them—Edgar Cayce, the Book of Revelation, Hopi prophecies, hidden Bible codes. I don't claim new information. I've only rearranged what we already have."

"What kind of information?"

"We're a species with amnesia," Tobias said. "We forget our history and repeat our mistakes. There's evidence of ancient technology—mechanical devices, batteries, stone monuments built with techniques we still don't understand. And then, through war and pollution, we lost it all. We bombed ourselves back into the Stone Age."

Claire raised an eyebrow. "Are you implying there were computers before the Stone Age?"

"I'm implying there's more to our past than we remember. Nearly every culture speaks of a great flood—a reset. Our species is older than the five thousand years of recorded history we cling to. Look at the Sphinx, Stonehenge, Machu Picchu—massive, precise, enduring. We can barely replicate them today."

"Are you saying the flood was a metaphor for nuclear destruction?"

"Some scientists have found radioactive soil layers," Tobias said. "It's possible."

Claire leaned in. "Even if that's true, how does it help us now?"

"The hope," Tobias said, "is that we save ourselves this time. That we break the cycle. We've destroyed ourselves before because we failed to see that we are one species. We couldn't live in harmony with each other—or with the planet. Or with the natural universe."

"The natural universe?"

"Yes. We are intelligent creatures evolving on a living world. And now we face a choice: remain divided by race, religion, ethnicity, and country—or cast aside those illusions and see ourselves as one. This is our crossroads."

"You wrote about this in your book," Claire said. "You suggested all developing species must face this moment. But now you're saying we've failed it before?"

"Yes," Tobias said, interrupting gently. "I implied it in my writing. But now, I'm saying it openly. Urgently. With certainty. We've reached this crossroads again. And we must act—now—to avoid repeating the same disasters. Our aggressive nature has outpaced our intellect again and again."

"But not this time?" she asked.

"Not this time if I can help it," said Tobias, realizing he was finally finding his true voice—and the purpose of his mission. His eyes locked with those of the audience, one by one. "Not if we can help it. If we come together, we may finally hold on to our technology and use it to build better lives. But the key is to treat each other as equals—sharing the planet respectfully with one another and with every living creature. We must become caretakers, not conquerors."

A man in the front row interrupted. "I beg your pardon, Mr. Sinclair, but I don't consider humankind to be merely caretakers. We're the dominant species. Animals and plants are lesser beings."

"That," Tobias replied, "is exactly the problem. We believe that because we have brains and dexterity, we have the right to dominate. But we've retained the aggression of our hunting past—quick to fear, quick to destroy. Physically, we've remained the same for fifty thousand years. It's our mental and spiritual evolution that's being tested now. We stand at the edge—success or failure. We can choose war, pollution, division. Or we can choose unity, compassion, and shared stewardship."

An older man stood up, visibly annoyed. "Sinclair! Your naïveté is astounding." He turned toward the door.

Tobias raised his voice, uncharacteristically. "Can't you open your minds—just for once? Whether by nuclear holocaust or environmental collapse, if we continue to believe in illusions like race, country, money, and sectarianism, we will cease to exist. We will become a failed sentient species. The Hopi, the Maya, and others have warned of a great cleansing. If that's our fate, then all I can do is help save as many souls as possible—even if civilization cannot be saved."

The man turned back. "Saving souls? Are you becoming an evangelist?"

Tobias softened. "No, sir. I'm not preaching. I'm trying to reduce the number of people who ignore the warnings. I want to help others understand the universe as it truly is—so we can continue as sentient beings in a stable civilization. And if we fail, at least some will carry the truth in their spirits. Understanding the universe is understanding ourselves."

He looked around the room. "You've heard of survivalists preparing for collapse. I'm talking about the survival of our species. And if we destroy ourselves, let our souls survive—with clarity, with truth."

"That's horrible!" the man exclaimed. "Are you preparing us to die?"

"No," Tobias said quietly. "I'm preparing us to live."

He paused. "But we need a shift—a radical shift—in how we see ourselves and our role on Earth. If that doesn't happen soon, the best we can do is enlighten as many people as possible. The more souls with positive energy, the greater our chance of survival."

Claire Jenkins pressed on. "You sound like an evangelist. You're talking about saving souls before we die."

Tobias shook his head. "You're missing the point. I'm using reason and observation to reach a conclusion. And based on that, I'm suggesting we create a plan—together—to save our species."

50

"But you were talking about souls and the end of civilization."

"Well, Ms. Jenkins," Tobias said, his voice rising with conviction, "even if we destroy our physical presence on Earth through aggression and hierarchy, we can still succeed—if our spirits awaken to the truth of the universe. This may be our last chance."

He looked into the camera. "Every time someone told the truth—that we must love one another to survive—we killed them. Jesus Christ. Abraham Lincoln. Mahatma Gandhi. Martin Luther King. Robert Kennedy. Medgar Evers. John Kennedy. Anwar Sadat. Indira Gandhi. Yitzhak Rabin. Benazir Bhutto. And those we didn't kill, we silenced—Paul Robeson, Sitting Bull. History is littered with the blood of truth-tellers."

Claire tried to redirect. "With all due respect, Mr. Sinclair, you're preaching to the choir. Food, education, green technology—they could be distributed evenly across the planet, in theory."

"Yes, in theory," Tobias replied, still fiery. "But only if we're motivated to share. I'm not just talking about resources. I'm talking about equality. We must treat each other as one species. We now have the power to destroy the planet. Any species that reaches that point must make a conscious decision: evolve or perish."

He raised his voice again. "I've used science, observation, and reason to explain this world. You can draw your own conclusions. But at least look at the facts. We have eyes—and we use them to judge. We have bodies— and we use them to kill. We've been ungrateful for the gifts we've been given. We ignore the truth."

The room fell silent.

Tobias, exhausted, glared at the crowd. "I guess no one likes being told the earth is not flat."

Suddenly, his hands began to shake. His eyes rolled upward. His body slumped, collapsing against the podium in a convulsive heap. His head struck the wood with a sickening thud, opening a gash on his forehead. He fell unconscious.

It was the first of many seizures Tobias would suffer—and it was caught on camera, recorded for all time.

At first, Tobias didn't know what had happened. His eyes were closed. The room was silent. Then his body stiffened. His limbs shook violently. But inside, he felt safe—wrapped in a cocoon, speeding through space like a torpedo. No wind touched his face. Instead, his mind filled with knowledge. Equations. Constellations. Geometry. Chemistry. A flood of information surged through him as his body convulsed.

It lasted less than a minute.

A woman screamed. Jimmy rushed forward, tears in his eyes, pressing a handkerchief to Tobias's bleeding forehead.

"Somebody please call nine one one!" Jimmy shouted.

"TS! TS!" called Jimmy, tapping Tobias's face.

Tobias began to stir, groggy and disoriented. The doctors would later call it postictal—coming out of a seizure. He murmured softly, to no one in particular, "We are one. The harvest time has come."

Claire Jenkins, no longer the hardened newswoman, knelt beside them. "Don't worry," she said gently. "An ambulance is on the way."

Back at the hospital, Tobias remained groggy on the stretcher, answering questions with only a word or two. Dr. Patel was on duty again. Jimmy, who had ridden in the ambulance, filled her in.

"What happened?" she asked.

"Before he blacked out," Jimmy said, "he spoke like I've never heard him before. He gave a speech—different from anything he's ever done. He talked about saving souls, about martyrs. It was almost... preaching."

"Has he ever been overly concerned with religion?" she whispered.

"Not really. He's always said he's spiritual, not religious. His lectures are usually about economics, race, and the future."

Dr. Patel turned to Tobias, speaking in a normal tone. "Mr. Sinclair, we must stop meeting like this." She smiled as she shined a light in his eyes. "It looks like you've had a grand-mal seizure. We'll need to run some tests."

She frowned slightly, the way any doctor would when their advice had been ignored. "You were supposed to take it slow. Speeches and book signings aren't exactly restful."

Tobias, still groggy, managed a smile. "The joke's on you, Doc. I didn't even get to sign any books."

Dr. Patel smiled back. "I see you haven't lost your sense of humor."

After reviewing his lab results and CAT scan—which showed no bleeding—she consulted with Dr. Jahmeer, the neurologist. The EEG revealed unusual electrical patterns and amplitudes. Tobias was readmitted.

Later that evening, Dr. Patel returned to check on him. Tobias was awake, sitting in bed, watching the weather report on the mute television across the room. Jimmy, exhausted, was half-asleep in the visitor's chair.

"Mr. Sinclair, you look much better. How do you feel?" she asked.

Tobias turned toward her slowly. His expression was calm, almost distant. "Better," he said.

Jimmy stirred, sitting up. Dr. Patel glanced at him, then back at Tobias.

"You were saying some unusual things earlier," she said gently. "Do you remember?"

Tobias nodded but said nothing.

Jimmy leaned forward. "It was like he was in a trance. He kept talking about unity. About survival."

Dr. Patel studied Tobias's face. "What did you mean by that, Mr. Sinclair?"

Tobias looked at them both, then back at the wall. "We must see ourselves as one to survive."

"As one species?" she asked.

He nodded. "If we can't discard our divisions—race, religion, borders—we'll destroy ourselves. We've done it before. We'll do it again."

Jimmy whispered, "That's what he said at the bookstore."

Tobias continued, his voice quiet but firm. "If we can move past this stage, we might evolve. We might reach the next level."

Dr. Patel hesitated. "You really believe we're that close to collapse?"

Tobias didn't answer directly. "We have so much further to go."

She let the silence settle, then said, "Get some rest. I'll see you tomorrow."

"Good night."

Jimmy touched Tobias's shoulder. "I'll be back tomorrow."

Tobias nodded, comforted by their presence. He fell asleep wondering what had just happened.

The next morning, he underwent a battery of neurological tests—an MRI, an EEG, and a parade of doctors in training. Dr. Jahmeer, the neurologist, gave no explanation, only a quiet reassurance.

"You'll be fine," he said.

Dr. Patel entered his room later that day. "The neurologist and radiologist found nothing wrong, and you've had no further seizures," she told him. "It may have been a rare incident, but we'll continue the antiseizure medication as a precaution."

Tobias's tone was grave. "Will I have more seizures?"

"I'm not certain."

"Can I go home?"

"Yes," she said. "But you'll need follow-up care in New York. Stress and fatigue may have played a role. Lectures, interviews—it's a lot."

"Don't worry. I'll be good." Tobias smiled faintly.

"Mr. Sinclair, this is serious. The first seizure was likely an impact event. This second one—we don't know. I'll contact your primary-care physician and coordinate your care."

"Sounds good to me, Doc."

"There's one more thing. You mentioned changes in your thoughts and behavior. I recommend a psychiatric evaluation once you're home. Our consultant found no cause for concern, but you've been through a lot. It might help to talk."

Tobias nodded, more somber now. He no longer saw the equations—but he understood them. He could see the patterns. The context. The meaning. But he couldn't explain it. Not yet. Not to her.

Only Jimmy would understand.

When Jimmy arrived near discharge time, Tobias was practically vibrating with urgency.

"They told me I can go home today," he said as Jimmy walked in. "Let's get on the first thing smoking back to New York City."

"I can't wait to get back either," Jimmy replied, subdued and weary. The past few days had reminded him of caring for his grandmother. He thought of Yolanda. Of the baby. Of everything waiting back home.

Tobias didn't notice. He was dressed, ready, already moving past the hospital walls.

"We've got work to do," he said.

Chapter 3: Objectivity

Tobias slept for much of the long flight back to New York. Jimmy remained by his side, willingly playing the role of bodyguard and caregiver—though by now, Tobias felt the only care he needed was Jimmy's friendship. It struck him how isolated he'd become since publishing his first book.

Now fully awake, Tobias broke the silence. "Jimmy, what do you think of the idea that I start a school—or maybe an organization? Ever since the mugging, I've been flooded with thoughts."

"Thoughts?"

"Nothing bad," Tobias assured him. "I'm not having irrational ideas. It's just... I understand things I shouldn't. Connections. Concepts."

"Like what?"

"Well, I told a nurse that Bill Cosby's wife, Camille, and their kids were related to Tom Hanks—and to Abraham Lincoln."

Jimmy blinked. "How would you even know that?"

"I don't know. I just knew it. Maybe I read it somewhere. But it wasn't about genealogy—it was about brotherhood. I wanted to prove that we're all connected."

Jimmy leaned in. "TS, do you think you're going crazy?"

Tobias raised his eyebrows. "If I am, it's a good kind of crazy. I just want to help humanity. I'm not losing my mind—but I might if I don't share these thoughts."

"You already give lectures. Now you want to start a school?"

"This is different. It's not about my books or past lectures. Something's shifted. I feel like I need to stop the tour and focus on this. We could use your teaching skills."

Jimmy chuckled. "Wait—the thoughts are in your head, not mine. If I'm teaching, do I get a raise?"

"You know what teachers get paid," Tobias said, smiling. "You'll probably get a pay cut."

They both laughed, and for a moment, Tobias felt light again.

"You'll be the first student," he said. "But I need your help. Some of these ideas are... out there. I'll share what I know, and we'll teach others. Get their input."

"What kind of ideas?"

"Since the mugging, I've had flashes—equations, concepts. It's like a continuation of that last lecture. I've been thinking about humanity's place in the universe. I believe we've reached this level before—and failed."

"I remember that. What equations are you talking about?"

"Just two, really. $E = mc^2$ and $c = \lambda f$. Energy equals mass times the speed of light squared. And the speed of light equals wavelength times frequency. They're simple, but they explain everything."

"How?"

"They show that everything—matter, energy, life—is interconnected. And the speed of light isn't just about photons. It's the rhythm of the universe itself. These equations can guide how we live."

Jimmy raised an eyebrow. "Guide how we live?"

"Yes. They reveal that we're already moving at the speed of light—interacting with everything around us. If we understand that, we can align our behavior with the natural universe. We can evolve before we collapse again."

"Collapse?"

"Look at Machu Picchu, Tiwanaku, Teotihuacán. Massive stone structures, no mortar. Some date back fifteen thousand years. What happened to the civilization that built them? We keep destroying ourselves."

"So what do we do?"

"We harvest ourselves."

"Harvest?" Jimmy frowned. "TS, that word's loaded. Slavery, concentration camps... After your seizure, you said, 'The harvest time has come.' Is that what you meant?"

Tobias nodded slowly. "I think so. But not physical harvesting. Mental. Philosophical. We need a new consensus. A shift in how we think. Reason and logic must guide us. The speed of light—it's not just physics. It's a metaphor for connection."

Jimmy leaned closer. "TS, I respect you. But saying you can explain almost anything? That sounds arrogant."

"You're right," Tobias said. "But it's not me. It's the perspective I've gained. Observation and reasoning—those are the tools. They help answer questions we've only speculated about."

"Like what?"

"How did we build the pyramids? Why did Homo sapiens appear so suddenly? Why did we become so smart, so fast?"

Jimmy shrugged. "Beats me."

"My new viewpoint helps me answer those questions. But more than that—it shows me that our survival depends on one thing: objectivity. Scientific reasoning. Observable facts. Logical conclusions."

Jimmy raised a hand. "Slow down. What are you talking about?"

"Actually," Tobias said, "what I'm trying to suggest is that we humans built those stone structures ourselves—but we don't remember. We blew our civilization back into the Stone Age and had to start over. Who knows? We're not the only intelligent beings in the universe. Even whales and dolphins might rival us."

"They just don't have thumbs," Jimmy said, half-joking.

"Jimmy, it goes deeper than that."

"What do you mean?"

"Answer your own question: why did our species appear so suddenly in the fossil record?"

"Actually, that was your question, TS. And yeah—it's still a mystery. Archaeologists have studied it for years. No clear answer."

Tobias relaxed. "But wouldn't you agree that my explanation makes sense? We have aquatic intelligence and simian aggression—and we can't reconcile the two."

Jimmy sighed. "You talked about all this during your last lecture. It sent you back to the hospital."

They fell silent.

Jimmy softened. "TS, did all these insights start after your head injury?"

"Yes. But there's something beautiful about reason and logic."

"What's that?"

"Anyone can use them. That's where the school comes in. My injury helped me see things we all should see. The school will teach how to solve problems through observation and logic."

"You mean teach people to think logically?"

"These thoughts won't leave me alone, Jimmy. I feel compelled to share them."

Jimmy paused. "Didn't your career as a lawyer end because of your first book?"

"Yes. But this is different. It's not a book—it's a way of thinking. A philosophy. It's mental."

"It's mental all right," Jimmy said with a grin, trying to lighten the moment. They shared a brief smile.

"It sounds like New Age," Jimmy added. "Maybe a new kind of science."

Tobias nodded. "That's it. The New Science movement."

"I'm down with that," Jimmy said. "But just one thing…"

"Yes?"

"What's the aim of this New Science?"

Tobias didn't hesitate. "To unify humanity."

"Unify humanity?"

"And keep us from destroying ourselves."

"Again?"

"Again," Tobias said, gazing out the airplane window. Raindrops streamed down the glass. "With New Science, we can finally see who we are—stark-naked reality. It's truth. It can't be disproven."

"OK, then what is the truth?"

"It's deep."

"I'm ready, TS."

Tobias leaned forward. "The truth is that we humans are just one of many species who've reached a sophisticated level of technology. But when you look at everything objectively, our true picture becomes clear."

"What is our true picture?"

"Let's hold that for the school. What are you doing when we get back?"

"I've got to check on Yolanda. Between school and working with you, I haven't spent much time with her. I think she's felt kind of neglected."

"I know what you mean," Tobias said quietly, thinking of his own family. He fell silent, reflecting on the school, the ideas, and the strange chill that crept over him.

The plane approached New York early. The captain mentioned tailwinds, prompting Jimmy to stifle a laugh. Tobias remained somber. It was Friday evening. The sun had set, casting the skyline in blue-purple darkness. Skyscrapers twinkled with light. Amber streetlamps erased the stars.

"Let's meet early Monday," Tobias said. "School's over. You're a free man now."

"You mean work overtime," Jimmy said, smiling.

Tobias smiled back. "Your baby's going to need some of that overtime money."

"Kids have a way of doing that," Jimmy said, happy at the thought of extra income.

The plane landed smoothly. They navigated the crowd, collected their luggage, and hailed a cab.

The taxi dropped Jimmy off first, pulling up to the apartment he shared with Yolanda in West Harlem, near City College.

"Seriously, TS, are you sure you'll be all right tonight?"

"I'm sure of only one thing," Tobias said with a smile. "And I'm not going to say what it is."

Jimmy stared at him, unconvinced.

Tobias sighed. "I'll be all right. You've gone above and beyond."

Jimmy stepped out reluctantly.

"I'll see you Monday," Tobias called through the window as the cab pulled away toward Brooklyn.

Jimmy entered the dark-green door beside the bodega. He climbed the wooden steps to the third-floor studio overlooking 145th Street.

Yolanda met him at the door before he could unlock it.

"Hey, baby," she said, embracing him with a long kiss. "I missed you so much."

Still holding each other, they stepped inside. Candlelight glowed around the room. The scent of rosemary-roasted chicken filled the air, mingling with vanilla from the candles.

Jimmy realized how much he'd neglected her—caught between finishing his degree and working with Tobias. Her body felt warm and soft. He didn't want to let go.

He whispered, "You missed me? I missed you, too. I missed the baby, too."

Yolanda looked down at her baby bump. "He missed you, too."

After dinner, Jimmy and Yolanda lay in bed, speaking in intimately low voices, as if to match the flickering candles nearing their end.

"I've got good news," Jimmy said, playing with her hair. "TS offered me more hours. I'll be making more money."

Yolanda kissed him. "I knew this was a good thing. No second job needed." She paused. "But I thought he was slowing down—especially after San Francisco."

"He is. No more lectures for now. But he's talking about starting a school or something. He asked for my help. He's inspired—but he's been acting a little strange since the attack."

"Strange even for Tobias?" Yolanda shook her head. "I never understood his books. Do you know what you're getting into?"

Jimmy sighed. "No. But I trust him. He's different—odd, yeah—but sincere. He sees the world in ways I've never heard before."

"Do you think he's serious?"

"Oh yeah. I start full-time Monday. Might even teach a little," Jimmy said, smiling as he rested his ear on her stomach.

"Our baby's going to have a professor for a father," Yolanda said, stroking his head. He drifted into sleep, and she cradled him, grateful he was home.

Monday morning arrived with a clear, bright midspring sky over New York. Tobias felt focused, energized. His apartment in Brooklyn, near Prospect Park, was Spartan—white walls, minimal furniture, a glass-top table in the dinette. His life had been devoted to writing, and it showed. Even his son rarely visited.

After breakfast, the phone rang. It was Mill.

"You're back! Why didn't you call me?"

"Didn't want to bother you. I knew I'd see you today."

"Coffee at our usual spot?"

"I'd love to, but Jimmy's coming at ten. You should come over, too. I need to kick around a few ideas."

"I've got to see how you stacked up against San Francisco."

"I'm still standing."

"I'll stop by later this morning."

"I'll be your barista. Latte to go?"

She laughed. "See you soon."

Not long after, Jimmy rang the doorbell—ready for work, ready for anything.

"Well, TS, I'm here to go wherever you want to go."

Though smiling, Jimmy studied Tobias's face, still wary of the changes since the seizure. Yolanda's concerns echoed in his mind. Stacks of books crowded Tobias's desk—clearly, he'd spent the weekend at the library.

Tobias sat on the sofa, facing Jimmy. "Let's get the show on the road. I've been thinking about how to reach people. You've got your finger on the pulse of the 'hood.'"

"You know I float around this city. What's your vision?"

"We need different approaches for different communities. Ads, maybe. Or a course at a learning center. Honestly, I'm not sure how to bring people in."

"Whatever it takes, TS," Jimmy said, half-serious, half-humoring him.

The doorbell rang.

"Don't get up," Jimmy said. "I'll get it."

"It's probably Mill."

Jimmy opened the door and smiled. "How's the graduate doing?" she asked, hugging him. "Has Toby given you a hard time?"

"No, but he's trying to wear me out."

She mock-scowled at Tobias. "Jimmy, if he gives you trouble, come to me."

Tobias stood, and Mill hugged him warmly. "I'm glad you're back. You had me worried out in California. Thank goodness Jimmy kept me posted."

"I'm just as good as new. Better than new."

"What's this about needing our help?"

"No more lectures. We need a home base."

Tobias and Mill sat on the sofa. Jimmy returned to the easy chair.

"Mill, I want to start a course. I need to bounce ideas off you—and anyone who'll listen."

Mill and Jimmy exchanged a glance. Something was different about Tobias. Mill, who'd known him longer, let him speak.

"What do you think of starting a course at the Downtown Center? They offer all kinds of classes for a small fee."

"As long as it's not a blackboard jungle," she quipped, though the idea intrigued her.

They wasted no time. Within days, they learned how to launch a course at the center—a place known for eclectic offerings: herbal medicine, yoga, science fiction, self-improvement. Tobias's course would be interactive, exploratory—not just lectures.

The first twelve students who registered were drawn by Tobias's reputation as a writer, though few understood the course's goals. They were a motley crew—disenchanted seekers, curious minds, readers of Tobias's work. Most were dissatisfied with traditional academia or religion. A few came after hearing about the author who spoke of seizure-induced insights.

They didn't know what to expect. Neither did Tobias. But something was beginning.

On the first day of class, Tobias stood at the podium, unafraid. He began where he had left off before the seizure.

"Thank you for taking the first bold steps into the unknown. This course is more than a new way of living—it's fundamental to how we see ourselves as a species. We must scientifically understand who we are to determine where we're going. That's what past civilizations failed to do. They saw only the immediate, the physical. They ignored time, space, evolution, and consequence. We never looked at the bigger picture."

He had their attention.

"In this course, we'll explore human history and prehistory. The pattern is always the same: we reach technological sophistication, gain the power to destroy ourselves, and arrive at a crossroads—progress or regression. But we've always failed the test. We bomb ourselves back into the Stone Age. If we could overcome our differences, we'd see ourselves as one species—and act accordingly."

A young man near the front raised his hand. Tobias nodded.

"What do you see as the real problem with human beings?"

"Our nature," Tobias said. "Our need for hierarchy— for leaders and followers. It's held us back. We're smart, aggressive, inventive—but we rely on artificial divisions to run everything. Schools, governments, cultures. We walk in lockstep. We've lost the ability to communicate across borders of language, country, and belief."

He sipped water, then lowered his voice.

"Have you heard of Tiwanaku? Or the Nazca lines in Peru—visible only from the air?"

"Yes," the young man replied. "There are mysterious sites all over the world. No one knows how they were built. I watch Unsolved Mysteries and UFO shows."

The audience chuckled.

Tobias smiled. "We can reason that humans built them. There's evidence of advanced technology long before our modern era. Look at Puma Punku in Bolivia—granite columns cut with precision. But we keep tripping over the same flaw: our aggression outpaces our intelligence. We fail to see the precious nature of human life. We fail to appreciate our ability to conceive, communicate, and build with our higher selves."

"Higher selves?" asked an older woman, skeptical.

"If we don't recognize our spiritual nature, we'll never evolve. We'll stay stuck—dividing ourselves by gender, race, religion, borders. We classify and separate based on physical traits and beliefs. The next step is to see one another spiritually."

A young man spoke up, louder than necessary. "Where's the evidence that all this happened before?"

Tobias gestured. "It's all around us. Pyramids in Egypt, Sudan, the Americas. We attribute them to religion, but we ignore how they were built—and why. Damascus steel, unmatched even today. The Library of Alexandria knew the earth was round two thousand years before the West accepted it. The Baghdad Battery. The Antikythera mechanism—a bronze Greek 'computer' that tracked celestial motion with intricate gears. Even the Old and New Testaments contain echoes of ancient knowledge."

A young woman asked, "I follow the Old and New Testaments. Do you believe in God, Mr. Sinclair? Was humanity created by God—or did we evolve?"

Others nodded.

Tobias's eyes gleamed. "Why must God and evolution be mutually exclusive? Why not say man evolved because God made it that way? Maybe the conditions that shaped us were guided by God. Who knows?"

"Are you saying God decides what happens to us?"

"Yes and no," Tobias said. "It depends on our choices. If the end comes from a natural disaster—a shift in the earth's axis, an asteroid, an Ice Age—that's an act of God. But if it comes from nuclear war, pollution, global warming—then it's our doing. If we stop polluting, stop threatening each other, and use clean energy, we can avert disaster. If our end is man-made, we have full control. It's up to us."

The room felt full, though fewer than twenty people were present. They rallied around him, each finding something in his words that spoke to their lives.

"I'm with you, brother," shouted a husky man in the back.

"Me, too," said a tall woman in a turtleneck.

Mill approached Tobias, whispering as the applause erupted. "I think you've just started something."

Tobias felt overwhelmed—sadness and joy mingling. He closed with quiet intensity.

"You may hear my message and yet not listen. Whether civilization ends by nuclear holocaust or a shift in the earth's axis, we must save ourselves and each other—or prepare for annihilation by our own hands."

The twelve attendees left with a mix of doom and hope. Tobias's words carried both despair and possibility. Word spread quickly. His lectures became the talk of the town.

The media blitz began. Tobias became recognizable. The train had left the station.

Over the next few weeks, his lectures at the Downtown Center filled to capacity. Even the video of his first lecture—and his seizure in San Francisco—went viral, adding to his mystique.

"Now I see how cults are formed," Tobias whispered to Mill as they waited for a new audience to settle.

The reluctant leader took his place, swept up by the current of events. He continued speaking at small gatherings, sharing knowledge—not signing books, but offering something deeper.

Over the next several months, Tobias's audiences grew so large that lectures had to be held in auditoriums and lecture halls. People wanted more—more insight, more answers—from the man who once claimed to predict the future.

At one lecture near year's end, an enthusiastic woman stood up. "You are ahead of your time. You're our Nostradamus. Our Edgar Cayce!"

Tobias, stunned, replied, "No, ma'am. I'm not ahead of my time. I'm here at the right time, in the right place. And so are you. So are we all."

Later that night, Mill asked him privately, "What did you mean? The right time for what?"

Tobias sighed, distant. "Sometimes I'm not sure. The words come to me—and I know they're true. People respond to the truth. I respond to the truth."

Mill leaned in. "If this is about truth, and you're trying to teach it, why not call it the New School of Truth?"

Tobias smiled. "I like that. Guess what? That makes you one of the founders."

"Are you roping me in?"

"The New School of Truth will teach the New Science."

Mill winked. "Whatever I can do. We're going to change the world."

The early days weren't easy. Tobias, Mill, and Jimmy met often at Tobias's apartment, shaping the New School of Truth. They decided to gear it toward adults, nonprofit, with tuition only covering expenses. Tobias was determined to share everything he could—with Jimmy, Mill, and later, Yolanda.

He continued lecturing at the Downtown Center, refining his topics with each new insight. His seizures became less dramatic—petit mal episodes, brief and subtle.

The medication didn't reduce their frequency, but he could function. He was grateful.

Preparing each lecture helped Tobias sort the jumbled thoughts in his head. He hadn't had another grand-mal seizure. His clarity returned in waves. But he sensed a plateau. Audiences were receptive—but not always moved to apply the New Science in daily life.

One cool evening, during a brainstorming session, Mill put it bluntly. "Hon, nobody likes to be lectured. It's like you're preaching."

"And we're the choir," Jimmy added with a wry smile. He'd brought Yolanda to the meeting—she was nearly due and feeling both happy and uncomfortable.

"I just had a thought," Yolanda said. "Why not bring the New Science to the people? Apply for a public-access cable show. You're already an author—you've got a built-in audience."

Mill clapped. "Hon, you're not just pregnant with a child—you're pregnant with ideas. Toby, you could take calls, bring new life to your lectures."

"Maybe the answers are the lecture," Tobias said, energized. "Who needs a podium? I'm not a preacher. Let's make it a Q&A. Let the New Science take on all comers."

Yolanda's idea took hold. The New Science program premiered on local public-access cable in New York. The format was developed by Tobias's inner circle—himself, Mill, Jimmy, and Yolanda. He called them the Four Musketeers.

Each week, Tobias gave a five- to seven-minute talk on a New Science topic to a small studio audience. Then he answered questions—from the audience and from callers.

The first show was challenging. Tobias spoke on using objectivity to understand the world. He hoped to spark meaningful dialogue—to help people rise above the causes and effects of human inhumanity.

The first caller was angry.

"Mr. Sinclair, I've read your books. You talk about forgiveness and reconciliation. Let's be real: How can African Americans forgive what happened to them? Native Americans? Jews? Russians? Chinese? Any group? How can you say, 'Let's forgive and start fresh'?"

Tobias answered calmly. "What's the alternative? Should we stay angry and keep fighting? Do enslavers still exist? Would you be angry at people who believed the sun orbited the earth? Or would you forgive their ignorance— even if it led to murder, witch burnings, executions? Can such atrocities be forgiven?"

"How can we forgive people who murdered out of ignorance?"

"How couldn't we?" Tobias said. "By fighting, we keep their ignorance alive. We're talking about forgiving the dead. The hardest part is forgiving the living."

"What would you suggest? Reparations? Take away inheritances?"

"If someone truly regrets inheriting a legacy of pain," Tobias said, "they might give away ill-gotten gains. Or create a foundation to help those harmed. It's part of apology, forgiveness, and healing."

An older man in the audience interjected. "Come on, Mr. Sinclair. That's not realistic. People won't give up inherited wealth—even if it came from slavery or theft."

"You're right," Tobias said. "Human nature makes it unlikely. But we must try. We must level the playing field—for our survival."

"Isn't that socialism?" the man asked, raising an eyebrow.

"On the contrary," Tobias said. "It sounds more like the New Testament—where Jesus told the rich man to give away everything to enter the Kingdom of God."

He continued carefully. "I'm not here to debate religion or politics. But I believe we must treat each other with dignity and equality. If we don't, we'll keep disparities in place and exploit the planet for a privileged few. If we correct the inequalities, we can move forward. Call it what you like—but without it, we'll destroy the progress we've made."

Mill and Jimmy, sitting off camera, weren't surprised. They'd grown used to questions about politics, religion—everything but science.

Tobias had wanted to focus on New Science theory. But he saw the bigger picture. The deeper meaning. The New Science touched every part of human life.

He was awestruck by that realization—and ready to follow wherever it led.

Mill leaned toward Jimmy and whispered, "He's getting better at answering these questions."

Jimmy nodded, never taking his eyes off Tobias, thinking of the seizure Tobias had suffered at the bookstore in San Francisco while answering challenging questions. He prayed it wouldn't happen again.

Another caller asked, "Mr. Sinclair, since you're African American, how can you talk so easily about forgiveness? Your people have suffered. They were slaves."

Tobias understood that people react most strongly to what they see. He knew he was seen first and foremost as a Black man—and that many audience members viewed him only in that context. Yet he felt the New Science transcended race, or at least transcended the implications of his identity. Still, he knew the issue had to be addressed. America's historical preoccupation with race—often buried, often denied—demanded it. Like President Barack Obama, Tobias knew he had to rise above it.

He answered carefully. "African Americans were not slaves. They were a people who were enslaved. One should never be defined by what others do to them. Would you identify a Holocaust survivor solely as a concentration-camp prisoner?"

The caller paused. "I've never thought of it that way."

"Many people don't," Tobias said. "Being African American is an analogy for all of humanity. Just as African Americans are a people with amnesia—forgetting their rich history—humanity is a species with amnesia. African Americans descended from many ethnic groups across Africa and beyond. Yet many think their history began with slavery. They forget the civilizations of Cush, Ghana, Mali, Songhai, Zimbabwe. They devalue themselves and their potential. So does society. That leads to low self-esteem and socioeconomic struggle."

Tobias could feel the room listening—really listening. He had their attention beyond race.

"Humanity, too, forgets its greatness. We must lift the veil of amnesia and remember who we are. We react to one another based on man-made concepts—race, country, religion, hierarchy. We're taught that civilization began with Egypt five thousand years ago. But it goes back further. Göbekli Tepe in Turkey is twelve thousand years old. It may reflect a time when people understood the true nature of the universe."

"The true nature of the universe?"

"Yes," Tobias said. "Those ancient people probably knew the truth—truth rooted in the New Science. But they used it destructively. They caused their own demise. Whether by war or disaster, we had to start over."

Jimmy whispered to Mill, "He talked about this in our meetings. I didn't think he'd say it publicly."

Mill whispered back, "I wonder how many people will think he's too far out—and how much of the audience he'll lose."

"Should we interrupt him?"

"Toby's on a roll," Mill said. "He's said too much already. But this is why he's here."

Tobias continued. "The problem now is that we're making the same mistakes—without even knowing who we are. We're technologically advanced but sociologically primitive. We judge by appearance—black or white, male or female, rich or poor. Then we react based on artificial beliefs about how that person should be treated.

"You are black because you think you are black—and imagine what that means. You are white because you think you are white—and imagine what that entails. You are male or female, Christian or Muslim, Australian or Brazilian because you think you are those things. But humans are beings with historical amnesia. We've forgotten who we are. We ignore our potential for higher understanding and live by 'eat or be eaten.'

"Just as African Americans have forgotten the great societies of central and western Africa, humanity has forgotten the great civilizations that existed long before written history. We are the species with amnesia.

"This amnesia persists despite the evidence—pyramids, temples, underwater ruins. We behave as if this is our first time down the technological path. Just as African Americans have devalued themselves and harmed their own communities, humans in general have devalued their worth and continue to harm each other through war, pollution, and poverty.

"We're destroying ourselves and the planet with only a fraction of the knowledge we once had. The time has come for humanity to receive the full information our ancestors understood—so we can make objective, logical decisions as a species. That full information is the New Science."

This was the beginning.

Tobias seemed able to answer any question—race, evolution, science, philosophy—through the lens of the New Science. The New School of Truth movement was born. It grew with each broadcast. Tobias explained the structure of the universe and its links to karma, religion, spirituality, and survival.

Word spread. His audience grew—from the curious to the convinced. Yolanda suggested webcasts to extend his reach. Tobias began fielding calls from around the world. The New Science program evolved into a series of interviews, talks, readings, and Q&A segments on satellite radio, the Internet, and cable television.

Tobias gained a following. Scientists and theologians challenged him—often baffled by his logic. Others saw in him what they needed: an accidental genius, awakened by a blow to the head. Tobias bristled at personal attention. He changed the subject when praised. He worried more about critics—those who dismissed him as fanatical or uninformed.

As the movement grew, Tobias became more reclusive. He continued hosting his show and teaching courses at the center. He asked people to use objectivity to answer age-old questions. His conclusions were often rejected—but never disproven.

He once told Jimmy, "Consensus is the key to success. If there's no consensus—right or wrong—there's no success."

Jimmy asked, "You mean consensus can change history? Like in Star Trek, when the Vulcans used logic to end their wars and revolutionize their society?"

"Yes, in a way it is similar, Jimmy," Tobias replied. "But the difference is that the New Science uses observation and objectivity to reach consensus. Logic is good—but objective truth is better. Right now, we humans haven't even agreed that we're one species with only superficial differences. We know it scientifically, but we don't act like we believe it. We fight and kill over artificial divisions. The New Science helps ensure that the consensus we reach is grounded in truth, objectivity, and reason."

"Are you saying it's not good to just use logic?"

"Well, Jimmy, logic is based on causes and conditions. The conclusions depend on those circumstances."

"So how is that different from objectivity?"

"They're related. You must use objectivity when being logical—but you don't need logic to be objective."

"Huh?"

"You observe what you observe. You draw conclusions based on what's seen—not on what's felt."

"You've lost me, TS."

"Whatever we observe in the world is a reflection of reality. It's not based on belief or emotion. It's based on objective, observable facts. Logic may be based on facts— or on logical feelings and thoughts. Objectivity is based solely on facts."

Tobias broke a slight smile. "My son, it is what it is."

His smile faded as he suddenly realized how much he missed his own son—and how Jimmy's presence helped to fill that void.

Chapter 4: Who Do You Think You Are?

As Tobias became more well-known, he was increasingly interviewed, questioned, and even interrogated by experts determined to dismantle the New Science. Some dismissed him as inconsequential. Others labeled him a fraud.

Mill had warned him during a meeting at his apartment. "The New School of Truth is growing, Toby. You're upsetting the applecart. The powers that be don't like being told their beliefs aren't what they thought."

"You know, Mill," Tobias said, "I'd like to gather them all in one place. Deal with their questions in one fell swoop."

"Then do it," Jimmy said. "Invite them to the studio. Let them ask whatever they want."

Mill nodded. "Maybe they'll see the New Science isn't a threat—it might even enhance their understanding."

Tobias smiled. "Okay, you two. Let's set the applecart back on its wheels."

He agreed to host themed programs, inviting experts from different fields—political science, physics, theology—to challenge the New Science. He scheduled the political scientists and lawyers first, saving the theologians for later.

"I don't want to open every can of worms at once," Tobias told Jimmy. "But I know I'll have to speak with the clergy soon."

Jimmy grinned. "Your plate's full enough. Ready for the lawyers and politicians?"

"As ready as I'll ever be," Tobias said, just before the program began.

Mill had scheduled the physicists for the following week. Tobias instinctively understood the political scientists' mindset—many were fellow lawyers. Familiarity breeds contempt, and their desire to disprove him was intense. Some feared he might seek office himself.

"You're a lawyer," they'd say. "Why not run for governor? Or president?"

But Tobias knew the danger of entering the man-made power structure. He didn't want personal gain from what he saw as a higher calling.

"I don't have political ambitions," he confided to Mill as the guests filed in.

Mill smirked. "You'd make a lousy president. No one could get a word in edgewise. Now go show them what you're made of."

The program began with cordial pleasantries and soft questions. But soon, the tone shifted.

One young attorney leaned forward. "Mr. Sinclair, this New Science of yours—it threatens everything I've worked for."

Tobias offered a calm reassurance. "It's not meant to erase your work. It's meant to expand our understanding."

The discussion intensified. The guests worried that Tobias's growing following might lead to calls for restructuring government itself.

"Would people abandon the current system?" one asked. "Would they demand a society built on the New Science?"

"No," Tobias said. "We'll still need structure. Government will still be necessary—to administer health care, education, sanitation, care for the poor."

A local assemblyman challenged him. "So you'd reduce government to delivering services? What about diplomacy? Defense?"

Tobias asked, "Defense from whom?"

"From other countries. From terrorism."

Tobias grew weary of caution. He was tired of tiptoeing. He had to speak from the heart.

"If everyone understood the New Science as clearly as we understand basic math, there'd be no need to defend ourselves—because there'd be no need to attack."

"What?" the assemblyman said, stunned.

Tobias continued. "If we taught the New Science in every classroom, we'd evolve—like when we learned to control fire, or cure disease. This is the next step in our evolution."

The room fell silent.

Tobias smiled. "Don't worry. This evolution is mental, not physical."

Another political leader stood. "How do you have the audacity to smile while talking about overturning the school system, imposing your 'New Science' on our children, and restructuring civilization? Have you gone mad?"

Tobias's smile faded. "The world has gone mad. Just look around. That's our problem. We always go mad before we annihilate ourselves. Again and again. This time, I hope we can avoid that fate."

The man sneered. "What's the next step? A world government?"

"Probably," Tobias said. "But not as you think of it. No hierarchy. Just a system to deliver services."

"It sounds like social—"

"I know," Tobias interrupted. "Socialism. Everyone asks that. But the New Science isn't socialism. It can't be imposed. It evolves naturally as people understand it. There are no disparities. People use objective evidence to make decisions—personal and political."

Mill leaned toward Jimmy off-camera. "He's not backing down."

Jimmy nodded. "He's finally saying what he really believes."

Tobias was met with silence again. He realized his words could be interpreted in many ways: as a threat to the existing order, or as the ramblings of a man untethered from reality. Perhaps it all depended on how many people were listening. Was the message more important than the numbers? Either way, the train had left the station. Tobias had launched it tonight, and it would not stop until it reached its next destination.

He had addressed the politicians with mental intensity, knowing the danger they represented and how fiercely they clung to the status quo. He waited for their next move.

The same assemblyman leaned forward. "How would you eliminate disparities among people—no rich or poor?"

"That's the point," Tobias replied. "There already aren't any real disparities. The ones we see are artificial—economic, ethnic, political, cultural, racial, national, sexual, religious. We create them in our minds and reinforce them by consensus. We've reached a stage in our evolution where we must recognize that everyone is equal and deserves a minimal standard of living. If we don't get past that hurdle, we'll remain divided—unable to reconcile the imperfections within our species."

"Imperfections?"

"One imperfection is our aggressive nature," Tobias said. "We could focus on correcting that instead of wasting energy on maintaining artificial political structures."

A lawyer interrupted. "Are you saying we should disband the government?"

"No," Tobias said calmly. "Aggression may have served us when we hunted for survival, but now it hinders progress. Our evolution is like a bad movie on repeat. Like *Groundhog Day*, we reach a certain level of technology, then self-destruct—usually through political or religious aggression—and start over. Look at Easter Island. When the trees were gone and the statues could no longer be built, their society collapsed into violence and human sacrifice."

He paused. "We've been through this before. We divide ourselves into artificial groups and fight over contrived differences."

The assemblyman smirked. "Sometimes, Mr. Sinclair, one plus one doesn't equal two."

"Really?" Tobias raised an eyebrow.

"Yes. If you have power, you can make the numbers say whatever you want—even if it means bending the truth. Just watch the news. Hatred and violence twist facts and justify the killing of innocents."

Tobias nodded solemnly. "Then let the unbent truth set us free."

The assemblyman pressed further. "Ministers, rabbis, imams, priests—they've all said the same thing. How are you different from any other preacher telling people to be nice?"

"That's just it," Tobias said. "I'm not a minister. What I'm saying has more to do with science and politics than religion."

"What do you mean?"

"It's not just about kindness. It's about shifting how we objectively view ourselves. Every human being is equally valuable—regardless of race, gender, nationality, orientation, or belief. These divisions are illusions."

"And you think that will end political violence and inequality?"

"I know it sounds unusual," Tobias said. "But we must see ourselves—and each other—as waves of energy. Not just bodies. Not just labels. If we adopted that view, political turmoil would seem pointless."

He paused. "Thoughts and behaviors are waves. Kindness is a positive wave. Cruelty is a negative wave. That's how karma works."

"Karma? You mean punishment and reward?"

"More accurately, karma is cause and effect—of thoughts and actions," Tobias explained. "In physics and in the New Science, positive and negative waves can cancel each other out. Positive waves create more positivity. Negative waves breed more negativity. Human energy behaves the same way."

A skeptical voice cut in. "Mr. Sinclair, this proves nothing. It's not political science. People make good and bad choices every day."

"That's exactly my point," Tobias said. "You and I make choices. Government is just people. Every organization is made of individuals. But we've built structures—laws, hierarchies—that seem more valuable than the people they're meant to serve. That's a mistake. No government is more valuable than a human life."

He leaned forward. "Decide for yourself whether you were taught correctly. Question whether we can make better choices—as individuals and as a society. Question whether every person is of equal value. Whether your government serves or harms. Whether poverty, famine, and violence are acceptable. Whether we should share the planet fairly and treat every member of our species as an equal."

An elderly female attorney spoke up. "Isn't it naive to think the developed world would give up its wealth and power to help the rest?"

"You're right," Tobias said. "That would be naive. But I'm not asking for surrender—I'm asking for reflection. Each person must question their beliefs. Who are we as a species? Where are we going? Why divide ourselves into countries, races, religions—and fight over illusions we created by consensus?"

"Are you suggesting we overthrow the government? Or create a world government?"

"I'm suggesting something bigger," Tobias said. "Each of us has a government in our own mind. I'm suggesting we govern ourselves. Formal governments wouldn't need to be overthrown—they'd evolve naturally, guided by objectivity and practicality. Why must we be governed at all? Sure, the nuts and bolts of society must function. But do we need a paternalistic structure dictating every move?"

He paused. "The real answer is that we must treat each person with equal value—and finally unite as one species."

The elderly lawyer frowned. "How could someone of your education and years be so naive?"

Tobias smiled slyly. "Maybe we should all be a little naive. Instead of assuming the worst, why not give each other the benefit of the doubt? Sometimes, our education and experience get in the way of true progress."

Tobias realized he'd given too much time to the politicians and lawyers. He was reluctant to delve further into concepts still forming in his mind.

"I must move on," he said respectfully.

He took a call from a listener while the lawyer sat down, still visibly irritated.

"I enjoy your show every week," said the woman caller. "I like when you bring in experts. I'm just an office worker, but I have a question. Most of us know about the New Science philosophy, Mr. Sinclair. How is it different from New Age ideas—and why is it so important?"

"The New Science will lead to the New Age," Tobias replied. "Its answers will help us change society for the better. It's important because I believe we won't survive— maybe not even as a species—if we keep viewing ourselves as separate."

"How?"

"With the New Science, we'd see each person as a precious equal. Once we truly understood that, terrorism would be unthinkable. Killing, torture, war—they'd be beneath us."

Mill signaled that Tobias was out of time. He ended the show feeling frustrated. The political scientists and attorneys hadn't grasped the core of his message. They couldn't imagine a world beyond their familiar lattice of hierarchy and control.

For the next seven days, Tobias secluded himself in his apartment, reading physics textbooks. He didn't meet with Mill or Jimmy. Despite the insights from his seizures, he felt unprepared for the physicists and cosmologists. A quiet unease settled over him.

Yet he knew physics was the foundation of the New Science. His dreams and visions continued—equations like $E = mc^2$ and $c = \lambda f$ swirled in his mind. Though he had no formal training, his childhood affinity for numbers and his intuitive grasp of complex relationships gave him confidence. Eventually, he felt ready.

On the day of the program, Tobias entered the studio alone and sat at the conference table. Mill stood off to the side, resisting the urge to say, "Long time no see." Jimmy remained unseen in the back of the room.

Three physicists—two sent by the American Physical Society—sat among the small studio audience. They were poised, confident, and skeptical. They believed the New Science lacked a physical basis and saw Tobias as an outsider with no scientific credentials.

Tobias cut to the chase.

"Physics is where the New Science becomes fascinating. There is a physical, reproducible basis for it. Your current theories aren't far off—$E = mc^2$ is still $E = mc^2$. I'm simply suggesting a shift in perspective. The data may be correct. It's how we interpret it that may need adjusting."

The physicists exchanged skeptical glances. More than any other group, they felt threatened.

"What do you mean, Mr. Sinclair?" asked a man who identified himself as a university professor.

"Don't worry—we're on the same side," Tobias said. "Your theories, including string theory, are based on observation. They're generally correct. I'm suggesting we interpret those observations differently."

He continued, undeterred. "Einstein's $E = mc^2$ describes mass-energy equivalence—energy contained in mass, even when stationary. But I propose we examine the total energy (E) involved when two masses interact near the speed of light (c). Why is c squared? Because two masses are interacting—each moving near the speed of light relative to the other. Whether subatomic or cosmic, their interaction produces energy. The outcomes vary—from no reaction to nuclear explosion to the creation of life."

He paused. "The New Science can help explain everything—from planetary motion to subatomic behavior. It's a new theory of everything."

Tobias recognized the man in the front row. Professor Thaddeus Stokes. They'd clashed in Denver during

Tobias's last book tour. Stokes had practically called him a fraud.

Tobias frowned slightly. This time, he felt less threatened—Mill and Jimmy were nearby.

Stokes stood. "Mr. Sinclair, you've gone too far. We physicists have worked on string theory and other models for decades. We're still searching for a unified theory. Even Einstein couldn't solve it. How can you claim to have the answer? Who do you think you are?"

Tobias responded with clarity born from his seizures and the quiet aftermath of insight.

"Einstein's relativity explains large-scale phenomena—planets, galaxies. Quantum theory explains the small—atoms, subatomic particles. For decades, physicists have struggled to unify these realms. String theory suggests that all matter is composed of vibrating strings—different forms based on energy levels."

"Yes," Stokes said. "That's a simplified explanation."

Tobias nodded. "And it's nearly correct. But it's not just about knowledge—it's about perspective. Let's revisit $E = mc^2$. If we see energy as the result of interactions between two masses near the speed of light, then c^2 represents the energy radiating from both masses. That's why c must be squared."

He leaned forward. "But it goes deeper."

"How so?" asked Stokes.

"Our universe seems enormous, doesn't it?"

"Of course."

"Telescopic methods measure the observable universe at nearly fourteen billion light-years in every direction. That's how long it took for light from the Big Bang to reach us. Fourteen billion years of travel—just to be seen."

"Yes, Mr. Sinclair," said Stokes, "it's also why we estimate the universe to be nearly fourteen billion years old. More precisely, the observable universe is thought to be 13.82 billion years old. Due to its expansion, it's estimated to span 91 billion light-years in diameter—though the full size may be infinite."

"Well," Tobias said, "as big and old as it is, the entire universe may behave like a subatomic particle."

"You mean it travels near the speed of light?"

"Yes. If the observable universe is moving at 186,000 miles per second and spans 91 billion light-years—roughly 546 sextillion miles—it behaves like a wave. The length of the wave determines its frequency when traveling at light speed."

"What do you mean by 'frequency' of the universe?"

"Frequency refers to the regularity of the universe's wave-like motion within a larger space. Imagine universes as snakes—shorter ones move faster, with higher frequency. Our universe has its own frequency, based on its length and speed. Frequency equals speed divided by wavelength. An observer in a larger universe would perceive our universe as traveling at roughly 3.4×10^{-19} cycles per second. At that frequency, our universe would appear as electromagnetic radiation—light. In this way, our universe behaves like a subatomic particle."

Stokes leaned back, intrigued.

Tobias continued, "Professor Stokes, does this make sense? If our entire universe existed as an electron in a carbon atom in another universe, many theories in physics would align more easily. The New Science doesn't change physics—it explains it."

"Please elaborate," Stokes said, now speaking for the room.

"This relates to the challenge of unifying the physics of large and small objects. Planets and galaxies follow Einstein's general relativity—macroscopic laws tied to time and gravity."

"Yes."

"But atoms behave differently. On the quantum scale, events occur rapidly. We can't pinpoint an electron's location—only probabilities. That's quantum theory. The unification between quantum and relativity emerges when we view our universe as an electron in a larger universe."

"Our universe is an electron in a greater universe?" Stokes asked.

"Yes. From that larger universe's perspective, our universe behaves like an electron—subject to quantum laws. And that larger universe may itself be an electron in an even greater universe. It's recursive. One universe follows relativity, the smaller one follows quantum mechanics. It's all relative—no pun intended."

Tobias smiled. "But the smaller universe can't perceive the larger one. It only senses its influence—its nuances."

Stokes, now entranced, softened. "Fascinating. So a person in the smaller universe appears as a subatomic particle to someone in the larger universe. Quantum rules below, relativity above."

"Yes. But remember, the smaller-universe person could be governed by relativity from the perspective of someone in a quantum universe within the smaller universe."

Stokes blinked. "I don't quite follow. Can you give an example?"

"Think of us as fish in an aquarium," Tobias said. "The fish isn't aware of the water. Our universe is the fish. The Greater Universe is the aquarium. The fish doesn't see the glass—but the bubbles and currents affect its life. Some call this fate. Others call it universal intelligence. Some call it God."

"So you're saying the subtleties in our lives are influenced by energies from another universe—like bubbles in an aquarium?"

"Yes," Tobias said, watching Stokes's expression hover between awe and confusion. "We may be perceived by those in the larger universe as electrons in a carbon atom—just as we might perceive another universe the same way."

"So every electron in a carbon atom in our bodies could be a separate universe?" asked another physicist.

"Yes. We struggle to perceive the larger universe, just as we fail to recognize electrons as universes themselves. The fish can't see the aquarium. The aquarium sees the fish. The universe sees the atom. The atom doesn't see the universe."

Tobias paused, eyes twinkling. "When was the last time an electron in a carbon atom said to you, 'We're here! Be good to us'?"

The studio erupted in laughter. The tension broke. Tobias chuckled with them.

"Of course it sounds ridiculous," he said. "But think about it. The atom can't perceive the universe. Yet the universe perceives the atom. We face the same challenge—trying to connect with our larger universe. And the only place where quantum theory and relativity seem to converge is in a black hole."

"A black hole?" Stokes asked. "Are you saying we could travel through one to reach the larger universe? Wouldn't we be crushed by gravity?"

"Well," Tobias said, "a black hole is a collapsed star—its gravity so intense that not even light escapes. That gravity behaves like the strong nuclear force that holds atoms together. A large object begins to act like a small one. Quantum physics and relativity converge. The black hole becomes a window into the Greater Universe."

A woman in the audience asked, "If that's true, could we use a black hole—or a wormhole—to travel there?"

"A black hole, yes. A wormhole, no. A wormhole connects two points within the same universe. A black hole connects two different universes. If the universe were a house, a wormhole takes you to another room. A black hole takes you to another house."

She blinked. "Huh?"

Sensing their dismay, Tobias leaned in. "Let me give you an example. If you're traveling through a black hole and you're ninety percent on our side of its center, then ninety percent of the physics would involve general relativity, and ten percent would involve quantum physics—from our universe's perspective. But if you're ninety percent on the larger universe's side, then the ratio flips—ten percent relativity, ninety percent quantum."

The physicists nodded. Even Stokes leaned back, receptive.

"Here's where it gets intriguing," Tobias continued. "From our viewpoint, someone mostly in the larger universe appears ninety percent atom, ten percent person. But from the larger universe's perspective, they appear ninety percent person, ten percent atom. Nothing is crushed—it's a transition. From macroscopic to microscopic. From universe to electron."

"When the person is fully within the larger universe," he added, "they're perceived as one hundred percent person there—and one hundred percent atom here."

"I see," said Stokes, now less skeptical.

"Actually," Tobias said, "when someone enters the larger universe, they perceive us as subatomic particles. They disappear from our 'house' and enter a new world where our universe is just another particle."

102

"Shades of Alice in Wonderland," Stokes murmured.

"Yes," Tobias smiled, "but now we have the physics to back it up. All evidence points to a continuum—where we may be simultaneously infinitely large and infinitely small. We're a tiny part of the continuum, but we perceive ourselves as vast. Someone in the Greater Universe may see us as an electron. We are both small and large at the same time."

The room fell silent.

Tobias sighed. "It's okay to have differences. But we must unite behind truth. It should bring us together—and help us evolve."

A physicist tried to corner him. "Then how do you explain dark matter and dark energy?"

Tobias didn't flinch. "The New Science offers a feasible explanation. Both are results of our universe's movement. Think of riding in a car with the windows down. The car is our universe. The wind is the larger universe surrounding us. Dark matter and energy are like that wind—interacting with our quantum universe. Just as a car feels drag from Earth's atmosphere, our universe feels the influence of the larger one. That's why dark matter and energy are ubiquitous."

He scanned the room. "It goes deeper. If someone stood in the universe surrounding our Greater Universe— call it the Greater Universe's Greater Universe—they might perceive our entire cosmos as a subatomic particle. Some call this space-time. But it's more than four dimensions.

It's a continuum of infinitely interacting Greater Universes."

Then came a phone call. Tobias was startled to hear a child's voice.

"Why are you grown-ups arguing?" asked a girl, sounding about ten. "Doesn't outer space just go on forever?"

Tobias smiled. "You're right. The universe can go on forever—that's a function of time. But many people resist new ways of seeing the world. It's like we have to start over from scratch. That makes them uncomfortable."

"What angle should they see it from?"

"They need to understand that our world can be both the biggest and the smallest thing at the same time."

"How do you mean?"

"Let's say the Earth is a ball. There are other balls— like the moon, planets, and sun. There are countless stars and their planets. All the space and stars we can see—and even those we can't—make up the universe. Are you with me?"

"Yeah."

"Well, here's the tricky part. The whole universe is a ball too—and it exists as a tiny ball inside another universe."

"What?"

104

"We live on a ball inside a bigger ball. But that bigger ball looks tiny when viewed from outside."

A woman's voice in the background asked, "Is Mr. Sinclair confusing you, dear?"

"No, Mommy. We're talking about balls!"

"Balls?"

"Universe balls!"

The girl returned to the line. "I get it, Mr. Sinclair. We live on a ball called Earth inside a bigger ball called the universe. And our universe ball can squeeze down to almost nothing if it's inside an even bigger ball."

"Out of the mouths of babes," Mill whispered to Jimmy.

Tobias beamed. "You're right. Many grown-ups don't understand things the way you do. What's your name?"

"Elisa."

"How old are you?"

"Almost ten," she said proudly.

"Well, Elisa, by the time you're a teenager, you'll understand the world better than any generation before you. Keep listening."

Turning back to the audience, Tobias said, "Our universe probably 'squeezes down' because, as a subatomic particle, it's interacting with its larger universe near the speed of light. This may be what's on the other side of a black hole—where light can't escape. It's also why photons behave as both waves and particles. Your universe becomes a subatomic particle."

Stokes spoke again. "Okay, Mr. Sinclair. If our universe is a subatomic particle, then it's part of an atom in some kind of parallel universe. What kind of atom?"

Tobias smiled. "That's the beautiful part. I wouldn't call it a parallel universe—it's simply the larger universe in which ours exists as a particle. And the atom? Most likely a carbon atom. Not just any carbon atom—a living one."

"A living carbon atom?" Stokes repeated.

"Yes," Tobias said. "The atom of carbon most likely resides in a living creature in that universe. And since we're made of living carbon, we're probably similar to the structure of the universe itself. We are of living carbon— and our universe is of living carbon."

"So, in theory, the universe should be teeming with life," said Stokes.

"Probably," Tobias continued. "And it also explains the Big Bang. Believe it or not, it's still happening. If our universe is a subatomic particle—like an electron—it appears and disappears in time and space, just like any other quantum particle. What we call the Big Bang is the appearance of that particle. What we call the end of the universe is its disappearance. Our electron-universe flickers into existence at a location within a living carbon atom."

"What do you mean?"

"Our universe behaves like a quantum particle. What we perceive as the Big Bang is, from another universe's perspective, the appearance of a subatomic particle. That means every subatomic particle in our universe could be someone else's universe."

He paused. "Scientists have long observed that energy can become matter—pair production—and matter can become energy—mass-energy equivalence. That's why $E = mc^2$ means matter and energy are the same. It's also why you're composed of both—your body is matter, your spirit is energy."

"Wait a minute," said another physicist. "Are you saying universes and subatomic particles are the same?"

"They behave the same way," Tobias replied. "Subatomic particles operate on a different level. We can't predict their location. Now you see it, now you don't. That's quantum physics. If our universe is a subatomic particle, then its creation—the Big Bang—is simply its appearance in a seemingly random location."

"Seemingly random?"

"Yes. Each location is a possibility on the time-space continuum. There are infinite universes—not just based on the number of particles, but on the infinite possibilities of their location in time and space."

"Universes and particles appear and disappear?"

"Yes. Matter and energy are interchangeable. Particle-antiparticle collisions can convert mass into energy—annihilation. Energy can become matter—pair production."

Stokes leaned forward. "Tobias Sinclair, you've reduced us to a reaction in physics. Is that all we are in your New Science?"

"No," Tobias said gently. "Here's the kicker: We think the Big Bang happened fourteen billion years ago. But we don't realize it's still happening. We're inside the particle—we're part of the electron. From our perspective, the universe seems enormous because we're so small within it. Our perception of time is slower for the same reason."

He continued. "Every living carbon atom contains a nearly infinite number of subatomic particles—appearing and disappearing, just like our universe. We think our universe is vast and expanding because we're made of its matter. But from the outside, it's just a speck—a particle flickering into existence. Still, from our perspective, it's a powerful Big Bang."

"We look out into space and think our universe is huge. But that's the mistake. It's actually quite small. It's a subatomic particle. We are travelers in time and space—and we can use our thoughts to shape our environment."

"So every electron in a carbon atom is a universe?" asked Stokes. "And every universe is an electron in another carbon atom?"

"I'm suggesting we move from the old science—four dimensions: length, width, depth, and time—to the New Science, which includes a fifth dimension: interconnected universes."

"How do we understand the fifth dimension?" Stokes asked.

Tobias smiled. "Go to one of their concerts."

"This is serious."

"It's simple. Our universe can appear as an electron in someone else's universe."

"So our whole universe exists as a tiny electron in another?"

"Yes. And the electrons we observe in our own universe could be entire universes themselves."

"Then there must be an infinite number of universes."

"It appears so. There are practically an infinite number of electrons. If we base our science on five dimensions, many things make more sense. We carbon creatures are alive—because our universe, also made of carbon, is alive."

Stokes stared past Tobias, lost in thought. "If we're alive because we're made of living carbon—and the universe is part of a living carbon atom—then the entire universe is alive."

"And if the universe is alive," Tobias added, "then what many call 'All That Is,' or God, must also be alive."

"So your New Science teaches that physics and spirituality are connected."

"Was there ever any doubt?" Tobias said. "Physics is part of God. We are part of God."

He stared ahead, voice calm and low, amplified by the microphones. "There is a continuum between science and spirituality. We must stay in touch with the perception of the larger universe—and recognize that it's part of a network of universes. This network is what I call the Greater Universe. Others call it the One. Some call it God."

He continued. "This network is what yogis, shamans, holy people, and avatars are connected to. Their message is always the same: use love as the basis of our beliefs, thoughts, and actions. We can help the larger universe through positive behavior. Even our sense of right and wrong is part of the energy of the Greater Universe."

"This is outrageous rubbish!" shouted one of the physicists. "Are you trying to use physics to define God?"

"No," Tobias said calmly. "God defined us."

At that moment, Tobias's eyes rolled back, revealing only white. His head slumped onto the table. Jimmy rushed forward to catch him before he fell.

It was Tobias's second public seizure—broadcast live and replayed on the evening news. But instead of shock, viewers were captivated. The depth and breadth of his insights left them wondering what knowledge might emerge next.

"He stumped the experts," became the phrase most often used to describe the encounter.

Tobias was taken by ambulance to a Manhattan hospital, with Mill and Jimmy by his side. Later that night, alone in his hospital bed, Tobias watched the footage on the late-night news.

He smirked. "Now I've made it to the big time."

At the hospital, Tobias was examined by neurologists and psychiatrists. Were the seizures causing his insights— or were the insights triggering the seizures? Could they be controlled with medication? Should they be controlled at all?

The doctors in New York were not like Dr. Patel in San Francisco. Tobias remembered her kindness, her warning that undue stress could worsen his condition. The local doctors seemed indifferent to the fact that he hadn't followed up with care. They wanted answers. They wanted to know the cause—and whether the seizures were linked to his revelations.

"They just want to pat themselves on the back when they find the cause," Tobias told Mill when she visited.

"Are you sick and tired of being sick and tired, Toby?" she asked.

"Well, when the seizures began, people saw me as some kind of oddity—someone who could explain things in ways few others could. I think the seizures made me see the world differently. Maybe the thoughts aren't even mine. That's what the doctors say. I'm just as surprised as you are."

"Toby, nothing surprises me about you," she said. "What do the seizures tell you to think or say?"

"They don't put thoughts in my head, if that's what you mean. It's strange—after a seizure, I see things as they truly are. Didn't I baffle those physicists?"

"You baffled them, me, Jimmy—everyone."

"Well, at least I'm not alone."

Day after day, Tobias endured a battery of neurological and psychological tests. After what felt like an eternity, he grew tired of the attention. He decided to leave—against medical advice. He didn't tell Jimmy or Mill, knowing they'd try to stop him.

He left without calling a cab. No fanfare. Just a quiet exit.

Outside, the cool autumn breeze brushed his face. He walked quickly past the farthest gate, turning right at the corner to avoid looking back at the cold gray building that had tried to define his fate.

Two weeks of his life had been spent convincing doctors—and the world—that he hadn't lost his mind. The scientists and critics had begun, again, to question his sanity. Or so he thought.

Despite the struggle, and the silence, he never imagined his final day of treatment would end like this— just walking out on a blustery, windswept day.

The maple and sycamore trees lining the sidewalk had surrendered their green to brilliant yellows, oranges, and reds. Dry brown leaves swirled in the street as he crossed the wide, nearly empty avenue.

At the bus stop, an elderly woman waited alone. The bus pulled up hastily to the bright-yellow curb line— perhaps the driver was running late. Tobias boarded slowly, stepping behind the woman, who was in no hurry.

No one recognized him.

He paid his fare and took a seat near the rear, where more space was available. He looked forward to crossing the bridge back to Brooklyn.

He stared out the wide window at the murky green water below.

"I have no home," he thought, as the bus lurched forward toward Downtown Brooklyn.

He closed his eyes briefly, reflecting on the convoluted origins of his present circumstances. His life had changed—for better and worse. But now, he had the chance to clear his thoughts.

And so began his journey toward a place he had never truly called home.

Chapter 5: A New Dawn

More people began to watch and listen to *The New School of Truth* program, which replayed earlier broadcasts until Tobias felt strong enough to return to the microphone the following month. During a brainstorming session at his apartment with Jimmy, Mill, and Yolanda, Tobias joked about the recent spike in viewers.

"Maybe they're tuning in just to see whether I 'fall out' again. People are something else!" he said, grinning.

Jimmy and Yolanda chuckled. Yolanda leaned forward, eyes bright. "You should stream the courses online, Toby. Let the whole world learn about the New Science."

Tobias paused, then nodded slowly. "That's actually brilliant."

Soon, his teachings were seen across the Internet. A new wave of followers emerged—not scholars, but ordinary people disillusioned with the world's systems. One young woman from the studio audience told Tobias, "I couldn't find satisfaction with science, politics, or religion. The New School of Truth makes so much sense to me, even if I can't understand it all."

Tobias smiled gently. "None of us can understand it all."

Since leaving the hospital, Tobias had suffered no further seizures. He realized he'd pushed himself too hard during that last program with the physicists. He briefly considered eliminating the Q&A segments to avoid triggering stress—but instinctively knew that answering questions was part of his calling. He focused on his weekly broadcasts, which continued to grow in popularity.

Professor Stokes was often in the audience, though he rarely spoke. He sat quietly, absorbing every word Tobias said. Once, Tobias caught a flicker of emotion in the professor's eyes—something between awe and urgency— but dismissed it.

A few weeks before Yolanda's due date, Jimmy left the studio early to be with her. He'd recently bought a used car and often gave Mill and Tobias rides home. That evening, Mill asked for a lift, and the two departed together. Tobias, planning to take a cab, found none in sight. He bought a newspaper and headed for the subway.

The platform was unusually crowded for 7:30 p.m.— likely due to a train delay. As Tobias passed through the turnstile, he spotted Professor Stokes standing alone. Their eyes met. Tobias hesitated, then chose to stand nearby.

Stokes broke the silence. "I hope you haven't taken the heated nature of our past debates the wrong way. I truly regret if I contributed to your seizures. But I had to be sure."

Tobias raised an eyebrow. "Not at all, Professor. Sure of what?"

Stokes hesitated. "I know it must seem strange that I attend so many of your programs…"

Tobias smirked. "I just figured you were my number-one fan." It was the kind of line Mill would've used to break the ice.

The train rumbled into the station, nearly full. They stepped inside and stood near the doors.

"I've been studying your materials," Stokes said. "Your approach to the New Science. I need to speak with you about the meaning of your work."

Tobias blinked. "You're going to tell me about the meaning of my work?"

"Your work is very important, Mr. Sinclair. More important than you may realize."

Tobias couldn't help the sarcasm. "Do tell."

Stokes leaned in slightly. "Your synthesis of science and spirituality is... enlightening. But the subway isn't the place for this. I'm getting off at the next station. Let me give you my card."

He handed Tobias a plain white card—just a name and phone number. No title. No affiliation. As the train pulled in, Stokes added, "I think I may be able to help you fill in the gaps," then disappeared up the stairs.

Tobias found a seat and rode to Brooklyn in silence, the card heavy in his pocket. At home, he called Mill.

"You'd better be careful, Toby," she said. "We've seen that guy at the programs, but what do we really know about him? I'm going to check him out online. Where does he teach?"

"Somewhere in Denver, I think."

Mill launched into her search. Later that night, she called back, sounding unsettled.

"There's almost nothing on him. No published papers. No university profile. It's like he doesn't exist. Are you sure this professor is safe?"

Tobias stared at the card. "Who can say whether anyone is 'safe,' Mill? Doesn't the New Science teach us to go with the flow of the universe?"

"Well, if you're going to meet him, bring Jimmy."

Tobias promised—but knew this meeting was meant for him alone. With Yolanda's baby due any day, he didn't want to disturb Jimmy. He trusted his intuition.

The next morning, Tobias called Stokes and arranged to meet at the Brooklyn Heights Promenade. As he hung up, he felt a strange clarity: if he was about to learn something big, he wanted to be surrounded by big things— bridges, buildings, ideas.

He arrived early on a cool midspring afternoon. The sky was a stark blue, dotted with drifting clouds. The harbor breeze was gentle, almost hypnotic. Tobias sat on a bench, watching baby carriages roll past, feeling a momentary peace.

Then a voice startled him.

"Sorry if I'm late," said Stokes.

"No," Tobias replied, collecting himself. "I was early. Have you had lunch?"

"Not yet. Let's grab a bite down the street."

They found a quiet vegetarian restaurant, frequented by neighborhood professionals. The ambiance was hushed—soft jazz, clinking silverware, the scent of rosemary and roasted vegetables. They sat at a table near the back.

Stokes seemed anxious but composed.

"Mr. Sinclair," he began, "you're probably going to find what I'm about to say hard to believe. But I must tell you what your work truly means."

Tobias leaned in. "I remember you saying that on the subway. You surprised me."

Stokes nodded. "The New Science is more important than you may realize."

Tobias's voice was low, but firm. "Important how?"

Stokes looked him in the eye. "Because it's not just a theory. It's a signal."

"A signal?" exclaimed Tobias, trying to avoid being too loud.

Stokes leaned in. "Yes. Just as Einstein's theories led to nuclear weapons, the New Science could be misused— with consequences far worse."

Tobias frowned. "I'm trying to help people understand the universe, not destroy it."

"I know. But knowledge alone doesn't guarantee wisdom. The New Science is powerful—too powerful for a species still driven by hierarchy and fear."

Tobias bristled. "Who are you to decide what humanity is ready for?"

Stokes hesitated. "That's the other reason I asked to meet. I'm not a physics professor."

Tobias sat back. "I figured that out. So who are you?"

"I'm someone who's lived both among humans and… elsewhere." He locked eyes with Tobias. "I need your word that this conversation stays between us."

Tobias hesitated. "I don't even know what I'd be agreeing to."

Stokes nodded slowly. "Then I'll trust your integrity. Have you heard of UFO abductions?"

"Sure. People say they were taken, examined, released. What does that have to do with—"

"Not all were released."

Tobias blinked. "What?"

"Some disappeared. Presumed dead. But they weren't. My parents were among them. I was born aboard a spacecraft."

Tobias froze.

Stokes continued, voice steady. "Earth has been under observation for thousands of years. The ancient structures you reference in your lectures? They weren't built alone. Extraterrestrials once lived among us. But they withdrew—tired of our violence, our divisions. They chose to let humanity evolve on its own."

Tobias stared, speechless.

"There are still humans within their society. Some, like me, were born there. We're trained to observe—to evaluate whether humanity is ready for the next leap."

"And you think my work is that leap?"

Stokes nodded. "Your lectures signal a shift. A species approaching universal insight. But the danger is real. You accessed this knowledge by accident—through trauma. You weren't meant to have it yet."

Tobias found his voice: "So what do you want me to do?"

"Slow down. Humanity isn't ready. If the New Science spreads too fast, it will be twisted by the old structure—used to dominate, divide, destroy."

Tobias leaned forward. "But if it can prevent annihilation—shouldn't I share it?"

"Not yet. Advancement in knowledge doesn't equal advancement in behavior. Look at history—physics led to bombs. The New Science could lead to worse."

Stokes's voice dropped. "Until humans stop seeing each other as enemies—by race, religion, nation—this knowledge is a loaded weapon. You must be careful, Mr. Sinclair. You may be humanity's last safeguard."

Tobias sat in silence, the weight of the moment pressing down like gravity itself.

Tobias nodded slowly. "If the divisions are gone, there'd be nothing to fight over."

"Exactly," said Stokes. "But humanity still clings to illusions—country, race, religion. The New Science could become a weapon in service of those old structures."

"You're saying people might use quantum-based tech to fight over things that don't even matter?"

"Yes. High-tech weapons for low-tech conflicts. The New Science teaches individual responsibility for the whole species. But right now, civilization still values group identity over personal integrity. As you've said in your lectures, the country creates the individual—when it should be the other way around."

Tobias frowned. "What does that have to do with me?"

"It's not just you. It's the timing. Normally, a species discovers the New Science after it's unified—no borders, no divisions. That's when the extraterrestrial community formally welcomes them. But you accessed this knowledge by accident."

"Accident? That mugger didn't hit me by accident."

"No, but the seizures unlocked something. You tapped into ancient knowledge—perhaps the collective unconscious Jung described. It didn't come from gradual scientific progress. It came too fast."

Tobias felt a chill. Mill's warning echoed in his mind. Was Stokes dangerous?

"You're not in danger," said Stokes, reading his expression. "We're trained to use our natural psychic abilities. You have them too. I sensed your fear. But our society doesn't believe in violence."

Tobias exhaled, still wary. "Then what do you want?"

"To advise you. After your injury, you began speaking truths you hadn't studied. We've monitored New Age thinkers for years, and you came closest to grasping the link between the physical and the spiritual. But now, you've gone beyond even that."

Tobias leaned forward. "So what are you saying? That I should stop?"

"No. Just slow down. You've already revealed too much. If you gain new insights, consult with us first. We're here to help."

"Sounds like censorship."

"Not at all. Maybe this is how it was meant to happen—a solitary man, a fluke injury, a leap forward. It's happened before. But every successful species that survived the New Science did so only after erasing artificial divisions and unifying as one."

Tobias shook his head. "You really think I have that kind of power?"

"Maybe not you. But the New Science does."

He paused. "You said our universe is an electron in a carbon atom. That kind of truth can reshape everything—or destroy it."

Tobias sat back, overwhelmed. "I should be freaking out right now. But since the seizures began, I know anything's possible."

Stokes stood. "All we ask is caution. Humanity's future may depend on how—and when—you teach."

Tobias looked up at him. "You've filled in a lot of gaps... but you've also created some deep canyons."

Stokes smiled gently. "Don't worry, Mr. Sinclair. You are not alone."

Stokes paid the check and left the restaurant, leaving Tobias still seated, trying to understand what had just happened. Strangely, he didn't feel shocked by Stokes's true identity or the fantastic tale he'd woven. Something gnawed at him—was any of it feasible? Yet from a place deeper than the seizures, deeper than his compulsion to cry out to the universe, Tobias knew the story could very well be true. And he didn't know what to think or say.

Should he keep this secret to himself? Or share it with the world? Would they question his sanity again? Could he trust Stokes? He was relieved he hadn't promised secrecy—only tacitly agreed to be discreet. After several more minutes in deep thought, Tobias left the restaurant and took the long way home.

He returned to a ringing phone. It was Mill.

"Well?" she asked, skipping any greeting.

"'Well' what?"

"What did Stokes have to say, Toby?"

Tobias paused. "Mill, we need to talk in person. Ask Jimmy to bring you over—we need a meeting."

"Jimmy just called me. He couldn't reach you." Tobias realized he'd left his cell phone at home.

"What's going on?"

"He's at the hospital. Yolanda's in labor."

"Okay, I'll meet you there—or better yet, I'll pick you up."

"You know," said Mill, "Jimmy was surprised you met with Stokes without him. Said he didn't know anything about it."

"That's right. I didn't call him. He had enough on his plate with the baby coming. Besides, it's moot—he had to go to the hospital anyway."

"Boy, Toby, you really slipped out of that one," Mill teased.

"Oh, by the way—you were right. Stokes isn't a professor."

"Tell me something I don't already know."

"Well… you're not going to believe what he told me. I'm not sure I believe it myself. I'll see you soon."

Tobias washed his face and took a quick shower. He was sweating from the shock of Stokes's revelations and the long walk home. He dressed in dark slacks and a blue button-down shirt, sensing that the miracle of life was about to unfold—and somehow, he was part of it.

He took a cab to Mill's house. She was waiting outside her building.

Tobias leaned out the window. "Hi, Mill. Get in."

"Took you long enough," she said with a smirk, slamming the door. "So what's the scoop on Stokes?"

Tobias glanced at the driver. "We'll talk at the hospital. I want Jimmy to hear this too."

They rode in silence, watching Brooklyn's brownstones give way to Manhattan's towering apartments. Tobias thought of the millions in the city—and billions across the earth—who might be impacted by what Stokes had told him, if it was true. He hesitated. *Be discreet*, Stokes had said. Would Mill and Jimmy think he was crazy? Would the world?

At the hospital, Yolanda was in the delivery room. Jimmy sat alone in the waiting area, clearly relieved to see them.

They hugged him. "The baby was turned the wrong way," Jimmy said. "They had to do a C-section."

He was anxious, unable to hide it. Tobias held back, unsure whether to share what Stokes had told him. He decided to wait.

Mill pointed down the corridor. "I'm getting tea from the vending machine. Want anything?"

"Nothing for me," said Jimmy.

"Just a regular coffee," Tobias added.

Mill left. The waiting room was softly lit with beige fluorescent lights. The furniture was modern, upholstered in greens and browns. No one else was there. The television murmured, "All news, all day."

Jimmy seemed more relaxed with Tobias nearby. He sat on the couch; Tobias took a chair diagonally across, a wooden table between them, scattered with magazines.

"How are you doing?" Tobias asked.

"I'm hanging in," Jimmy said, flipping through a magazine without reading it. Then he looked up. "TS, how did you handle it when your son was born?"

Tobias was startled. He rarely spoke of his son. He remembered mentioning David to Jimmy once or twice, but Jimmy had never asked. Now Tobias saw how anxious Jimmy really was.

He thought of David—now twenty—and how they'd grown apart since the death of David's mother. David rarely called, mostly staying in Philadelphia to care for Tobias's mother. Tobias felt a pang of guilt. He'd left them behind to chase something nebulous in New York. His mother, Rebecca, had forgiven him. David hadn't.

Just before Tobias's book tour, David had called.

"I'm stopping by Philly on my way back," Tobias had said.

"It seems that's all you do—stop by," David replied.

"Don't get too big for your britches," Tobias had snapped, masking guilt with bravado.

David had once told him he wasn't sure of his preferences—"intellectual, sensual, or emotional."

"What's that supposed to mean?" Tobias had asked Mill.

"If the boy's gay," she'd said, "let him tell you in his own way."

Tobias questioned himself. His absence had left David confused. At least David and Rebecca had each other. Tobias had only his quest.

Now, looking at Jimmy, Tobias saw David. He remembered the birth.

"Oh, I was in the birthing room," Tobias said. "Standing behind my wife. I told her to breathe—just like Lamaze class. She gave me a look that said, 'Fool, don't mess with me! I'm in pain!' I kept my mouth shut until the baby was born."

Jimmy cracked a smile. They both laughed as Mill returned with her tea and Tobias's coffee.

"Well, it sure sounds like you're having a good time. Did you get any news?"

"No, not yet," said Jimmy, becoming more serious.

The three of them settled into their seats, uncertain of what to say. Finally, Mill broke the silence. "Toby, I can't stand it anymore. What did Stokes say?"

Jimmy interjected, "Mill told me you went to see Stokes this afternoon. You still should've asked me…"

"Jimmy, now that I think of it, I'm glad I saw Stokes alone. You needed to be here with Yolanda and your baby coming into the world," Tobias said, looking at both of them. "If I hadn't met with him alone, he probably wouldn't have been as forthcoming."

"Forthcoming? What came forth?" asked Mill, almost whimsically.

Tobias looked at Mill, then Jimmy, unsure how to begin. "You're not going to believe this," he said. "I barely believe it myself. And I'm the one who met with him. I'm not totally convinced he told me the truth—it was so far-fetched."

"Far-fetched?" asked Jimmy. "That guy's been to nearly every book signing and lecture for months. He's questioned and argued with you about everything from physics to cosmology to sociology. What else could he possibly say? TS, this guy could be a security risk."

Tobias appreciated Jimmy's protective concern but stayed focused. "I'm glad we're all sitting down. I need to know what you think. Professor Stokes is not a professor. He said he's the son of two people who were—"

Just then, a nurse entered the waiting room and called Jimmy's name. He stood up, dazed, as if he'd forgotten why he was there.

The nurse beamed. "Congratulations, Mr. Rudolph. Would you like to see your new daughter?"

"My little girl... How's Yolanda?"

"Everything went well. She's fine. Please follow me. The other family members will need to wait here for now."

Mill and Tobias smiled at each other, touched by being acknowledged as "family." The three embraced silently before Jimmy left with the nurse. Tobias and Mill were left alone.

"Hi, Gramps!" quipped Mill.

"Thanks a lot," Tobias replied with mock sarcasm. Yet her joke struck him oddly, reminding him of the distance between himself and his own son.

Soon after, Jimmy returned with an expression somewhere between love, bewilderment, and joy. They all went to the viewing room, where little Grace lay behind the safety of the glass. She had a full head of dark hair that clung to her forehead, temples, and neck. She slept peacefully, as if she already knew she was loved.

Jimmy whispered, "She's six pounds and seven ounces."

Tobias smiled with pride. Though Grace wasn't his blood relative, he felt like the "gramps" Mill had jokingly called him. He thought of the world Grace would grow up in. He wondered about humanity's destiny—what Stokes had implied was still undecided—and how it might shape Grace's future.

They stayed in Yolanda's room until the nurse made them leave. Jimmy remained in the waiting room. Tobias and Mill took a cab back to Brooklyn.

Everyone was so touched by Grace that no one mentioned Stokes for the rest of the night.

Chapter 6: And the Walls Came Tumbling Down

Late the following morning, Tobias contacted Mill and Jimmy to arrange for the meeting that seemed to take an eternity to plan. Although Jimmy had slept very little after coming home past midnight, he wanted to meet in the afternoon before returning to the hospital to be with Yolanda and Grace.

"Let's make it at one thirty," said Tobias, hoping to give everyone enough time to collect their thoughts.

While preparing for the meeting, Tobias left his apartment to walk to the nearby park and botanic garden. Being in the presence of trees and grass helped his mind relax. He reflected on how humanity can cultivate nature but never truly create it—never reproduce the beauty, stability, and wonder of the natural universe. Finally, he felt free to think about the events of the past day.

Tobias realized he couldn't have taken Stokes so seriously unless he'd already glimpsed some of the same truths through his own writings and insights. The points Stokes had made weren't as far-fetched as they first seemed. The seizures had somehow opened Tobias's mind to a broader understanding. He grasped everything Stokes had said—and strangely, it didn't frighten him. He knew the time was right to use this knowledge for the common good.

Feeling sharp and focused after his walk, Tobias returned home to meet Mill and Jimmy. Mill arrived first, unable to hide her curiosity. Jimmy followed a few minutes later. They sat on the sofa in Tobias's sparsely furnished living room while Tobias took the easy chair opposite them.

"I know this is going to sound wild," Tobias began, "but when you give it some thought, it doesn't seem so outrageous."

Mill and Jimmy said nothing, listening intently.

"Mr. Stokes told me he'd been attending my lectures to study our progress in the New Science." Tobias paused, suddenly hesitant. He feared jeopardizing his fragile reputation. He didn't want to be dismissed for entertaining an outrageous story.

Mill leaned forward. "Well, Toby, spit it out!"

Tobias swallowed hard. His mouth went dry. He knew he was crossing a threshold. "Stokes told me he was sent by an extraterrestrial community—made up of alien beings and abducted humans. He said he's the son of two abducted people who live among the aliens."

Jimmy and Mill stared at him, then burst into laughter.

Mill caught her breath. "Oh, come on, Toby. You can do better than that!"

Jimmy added, "TS, you've been watching too much *Ancient Aliens*!"

Tobias laughed too, feeling a strange relief—as if a weight had lifted. Maybe he'd taken Stokes too seriously. Maybe he could view the meeting in a more realistic context. His laughter faded.

"Of course it's ridiculous," Tobias said, more to himself than to them. "But what if there's a small chance he's telling the truth?"

"Okay, Toby," said Mill. "What exactly did he say?"

"He said we came close to the truth with the New Science. That viewing our universe as an electron in a carbon atom could lead to new ways of harnessing energy. But he was worried people might abuse that power. He said past civilizations did—and it led to their downfall. He believes we're at a crossroads, and compared our situation to how Einstein's theories led to nuclear weapons."

Jimmy was no longer smiling. "Actually, TS, that kind of makes sense. But why you?"

"He said my books and lectures came close to the truth. But there's one big problem."

"What's that?" asked Mill.

"He said the extraterrestrial community believes we got the information by accident—and that humanity isn't ready for the New Science. He kept repeating that. We're not ready."

Jimmy frowned. "Do you believe him? Or did he seem a little… off?"

"Well, his story does explain a lot. The pyramids, Easter Island, UFO sightings, cave drawings. It lines up with what we've been exploring in our lectures."

"What does he want us to do?"

"Slow down our teaching," Tobias said, almost reluctantly. "He thinks we've already revealed too much."

Mill quipped, "Slow down? We're just beginning to speed up!"

Tobias nodded. "Stokes assured me that neither he nor his community will interfere. The responsibility is ours."

Jimmy asked, "So, TS, are you still doing the program this week on religion and spirituality?"

Tobias looked surprised. "What? That's this week?"

"Sure," said Jimmy. "You're supposed to meet with ministers and religious leaders. Did you forget?"

"I guess it slipped my mind. Between Stokes and that last seizure… and Grace being born…"

"Hey, shouldn't I be the one saying that? Grace is my kid!" Jimmy joked. "And it's my job to keep up with your schedule. I've got to earn my pay if Grace is going to college."

Jimmy stood. "I've got to head back to the hospital to check on Yolanda and Grace."

"I know," said Tobias. "We'll decide later if we need to make changes to the meeting."

"Not too much later," said Mill. "The program's at the end of the week. You know how intense people get when religion comes up."

Jimmy walked to the door, smiling slightly at Mill. "I'll have to let this whole thing about Stokes sink in."

"Me too. See you later, Jimmy," said Mill as Jimmy let himself out.

Tobias called out before the door closed. "Jimmy—it may be best not to mention any of this to Yolanda for now. She's been through enough stress."

Jimmy nodded and closed the door. Tobias and Mill looked at each other in silence, as if standing at the edge of a vast precipice, unsure where to turn. Mill broke the silence.

"You know, I forgot about the program with the ministers too. How are you going to prepare?"

"I'm just going to tell the truth."

"Well, Toby, the truth hasn't failed us yet."

———

Tobias felt well prepared for the special program later that week, where he would meet with ministers, priests, imams, rabbis, and other theologians. He sat at his familiar table in the studio, facing a small audience. Across from him sat a panel of eight religious leaders representing various faiths. Surprisingly, Stokes was not in the audience.

Tobias wasted no time. He threw caution to the wind.

"The most important thing to remember about the New Science," he began, "is that humanity must view itself in a totally different way. It gives us the opportunity to take a more objective view of religion, spirituality, and God. For example, as a Christian, my concept of God occurred through the teachings of Jesus Christ."

"You're a Christian?" asked one minister. "What kind of Christian? Protestant or Catholic?"

"Does it really matter?" Tobias replied. "I was born into a Christian family and identify my belief in God through the teachings of Jesus. A follower of Islam would understand God through Muhammad. A Buddhist through Buddha. What makes our species special is our ability to conceptualize God. But when we pit one path against another—Muslim against Hindu—we diminish both. If the end is God, and the means are our religious paths, then undermining another's path undermines the very end we seek."

The same minister pressed on. "Mr. Sinclair, how does your 'New Science' reconcile with your Christianity?"

"The New Science spans all religions. Yes, I consider myself a Christian, but I respect other faiths. Jesus was an avatar. His presence shaped history and helped humanity understand that we are more than our bodies—that there is a Greater Universe, a heaven, a God. He taught kindness and made us aware of the energy we put into the universe through our thoughts and actions."

"You're trying to teach us about Jesus?" the minister asked, astonished.

"You asked how the New Science relates to Christianity. I'm sharing my perspective. You're free to agree or disagree."

136

"I'm sorry, Mr. Sinclair. Please continue."

Tobias remained composed, speaking as if from unseen notes. "It's believed that Jesus spent His undocumented years—between thirteen and twenty-nine—in India, studying Buddhism, Hinduism, Jainism, raja-yoga, and other Eastern practices. He taught us the true nature of ourselves—spirit—and the universe—heaven. Acts of love and kindness strengthen our spirits and energize others. 'Everlasting life' refers not to our bodies, but to our spirits."

"Yes," the minister interjected. "And everlasting life refers to the survival of your soul."

"Exactly," Tobias said, sensing growing receptivity. "Negative acts—violence, injustice—diminish the energy of our spirits and others'. That energy moves away from the Light, away from God. That is death—true death."

"Death of the spirit is worse than death of the body," a female minister added.

"Yes. And here's where it gets interesting," Tobias continued. "Death, karma, and reincarnation are deeply connected. Hell may not be a man in red with horns and a pitchfork. It may be the suffering caused by diminished spiritual energy. If our spirit is too depleted, it may not reincarnate as a human, but as a lower life-form. To maintain our human spirit, we must perform positive acts and focus on God and the universe."

He paused. "To be given the privilege of understanding God, we must keep our spirit in a higher energy state. We do this by following the teachings of the enlightened— Jesus, Buddha, Muhammad, Moses, Confucius, Imhotep,

137

Krishna. Encouraging positive energy helps preserve our human spirits. That's how the New Science connects to all religions."

"So you're saying it doesn't matter what religion someone follows?" the female minister asked. "That it's all the same process of spiritual enlightenment through positive acts?"

"Yes. That's why we're all equal. Each religion is a different tool to understand God. But the goal is understanding—not the tool itself."

"Are you implying organized religion isn't important?"

"On the contrary," Tobias said. "It's very important. But the goal of understanding God is more important than any single doctrine. And if the New School of Truth fails—if humanity destroys itself—religions can still guide our souls. But if there aren't enough people left, our spirits may not reincarnate into human form. There simply wouldn't be enough bodies for over seven billion souls."

"How macabre!" exclaimed the minister.

"The New Science teaches objectivity—even when it concerns our survival and souls," Tobias said calmly. "We could save ourselves by living in harmony with the universe, using physics, karma, and energy as guides. But if we continue down this path—conflict, environmental destruction—we may annihilate ourselves. Our spirits won't reincarnate as humans because there won't be enough people. There'd be a long waiting list for a single spirit to inhabit a human body again…"

"Now see here, Mr. Sinclair," said an imam. "This is clearly all speculative."

"Yes, speculative but quite reasonable," said Tobias. "It is logical reasoning based on the New Science. Indulge me for a moment… After the destruction of most of humankind, many souls and spirits would be left in heaven, unable to reincarnate. It's reasonable to assume their energy and karma would determine their fate. A kind and caring person, aligned with God and karmic law, would continue to exist in a positive place—heaven. But someone who lived by lying, cheating, hurting, and killing would generate enough negative energy to be left in a place of suffering—hell. Our behavior, thoughts, and actions determine where we end up for eternity."

"This is the New Age mentioned in the Bible—the age to come. Those who continue to kill and hate will contribute to the demise of the species. And after annihilation, their spirits will struggle to enter higher energy levels. They'll be too depleted, and without human bodies to reincarnate into, they'll remain stagnant. If we can't save the species, we can at least try to save some souls."

"And is that where we theologians come in?" asked the imam, half-joking.

"Of course," said Tobias. "You were there all along. Humanity needs you. The New Science is just a key to new insights."

A Protestant minister leaned forward. "I've never heard a Christian speak the way you do. What do you consider yourself to be, Mr. Sinclair?"

139

"Reverend," Tobias replied, "each denomination is born of circumstances—causes and conditions. Even Jesus's life was shaped by the Roman Empire's expansion. As a Christian, I believe He was very close to God—His son. One might say Jesus was an avatar, deeply attuned to God's healing energy. He used that knowledge to guide humanity. Personally, I feel less religious and more spiritual, knowing Christ was influenced by Eastern faiths—just as Buddha was influenced by Hinduism."

"Are you saying Jesus Christ was a Jewish Buddhist?"

"I'm saying Jesus was spiritual and aware of the world. He understood the politics of Roman-occupied Palestine. He knew His actions could lead to harm, but He sacrificed Himself so we could understand the true nature of God and how to treat one another."

The ministers remained silent.

Tobias continued, "Aren't we all debating the same concept—God? Muslims, Hindus, Christians, Jews, Buddhists—we differ only in how we worship. But we all agree God exists and should be worshipped. Isn't that the point? We're killing each other over the same concept. Does it matter how we worship, as long as we do?"

"I'm talking about religion used to justify violence and warfare. If we embraced the New Science, we'd have no reason to kill in God's name. The violent actions of the unenlightened would no longer masquerade as devotion."

A cherubic priest asked bluntly, "Do you have any religious training, Mr. Sinclair? Seminary? What qualifies you to speak so authoritatively on God?"

140

Tobias answered calmly, "Aside from being a fellow human and child of God, my understanding of the New Science has helped me see God more clearly."

"How?" asked the priest.

"The New Science shows our universe is part of an infinity—both vast and subatomic."

"You sound like you're trying to quantify God."

"I'm not. I'm pointing out observations we can all see—if we keep our minds open."

The priest frowned. "Frankly, all I hear is godless blasphemy."

Tobias remained composed. "Blasphemy? I've said nothing sacrilegious. I feel I am a true Christian."

A second minister asked, "What do you mean by 'true' Christian?"

Tobias chose his words carefully. "I believe only in the direct words of Jesus Christ, as quoted in the first four books of the New Testament."

"And that's it?"

"That's it. Those are the words I live by. The rest of the New Testament was written by Saint Paul—his letters to the Romans. He was a follower of Jesus, just as I am."

One minister looked astounded. "Are you saying the rest of the Bible should be ignored?"

"No. I'm saying my personal belief is to focus on Jesus's direct teachings."

The minister grew irritated. "So the rest is just commentary? Saint Paul was just riffing?"

"Reverend, why create conflict where none exists? Saint Paul was devoted to Jesus. I see him as a fellow Christian. His words are as devoted as mine."

The room fell silent until a female minister spoke softly. "Mr. Sinclair, you've convoluted science and God so much I don't know where to begin. You're saying most of the New Testament is Paul's, not Jesus's, and that we can choose what to follow? No one picks and chooses from the Bible!"

Tobias had never considered himself religious. But the seizures had brought spiritual insights he couldn't ignore. He felt empowered to use scripture.

"Didn't Jesus say in Mark 7:8–9, 'You put aside God's command and obey the teachings of men,' and, 'You have a clever way of rejecting God's law in order to uphold your own teaching'?"

A priest stood. "Are you saying organized religion has drifted from God's Word? Who are you to say this?"

Suddenly, Tobias was overcome by a new understanding—like a seizure, but different. His eyes glazed over. His face became an unblinking mask of awareness.

He spoke solemnly. "I am here to help humanity live up to the ideals and standards that reflect our God-given intelligence." He stared ahead, looking at no one. "I am the Helper."

"The Helper?" asked an older minister.

"The Helper of the New Age to come." Tobias continued. "We are entering the End times. Group against group. Sect against sect. Wars and rumors of wars. The prophecy has come true. Either we end, completing the End times, or we evolve—becoming a globally successful species capable of seeing the forest of human existence, not just the petty trees of intolerance and sectarianism. My thoughts have much to do with Christ."

He explained, "You see, Jesus had omniscience; that is, He was a master of raja-yoga and reached a level of self-realization. He was at one with God. Many people have tried to reach that level, but none have fully reached the level of Christ. No one else has achieved the oneness with God that Jesus Christ achieved, and because of this closeness, He truly is the son of God. The good news is that we can all be part of the continuum—drawing closer to God by bringing yoga, especially raja-yoga, into our lives. We may not reach Jesus's level, but we can deepen our relationship with God, both individually and as a species."

"All Jesus and other holy people asked of us is to love one another and treat fellow human beings with respect, forgiveness, and kindness. As someone close to God, Jesus knew the nature of humans. He knew He'd be in grave danger once He began revealing reality and how the universe functioned. He spoke of unity. Yet today, we are just as divided and filled with hate as past civilizations we destroyed by our own arrogance. He knew humans didn't want to hear the truth: that love is the only way to survive as a species. He knew fear of change would provoke swift,

143

violent reactions. That's still true today—especially when the status quo is threatened."

"How dare you!" screamed the minister, his face contorted in rage. "How dare you speak as if you were sent by Christ Himself! You are a blasphemer!"

Tobias remained calm, still in a trance. "Why do you say I blaspheme when I'm only speaking from the heart?"

"I don't know what's in your heart, but it has nothing to do with Jesus Christ or Christianity as we know it!" the minister snapped. "First you were a New Age sage, then a scientific wonder, and now a religious zealot. You're quite the chameleon, Mr. Sinclair!"

"Forget about me as a messenger," Tobias replied. "Just listen to the message."

He looked at the minister and the other theologians. His trance began to ebb, like waves receding at low tide. "Your resistance to the New Science stems from your desire to cling to human-made rules. Your view of God is shaped by preconceived notions—not by observing the natural universe. The New Science paves the way for a new spirituality—"

A minister with piercing eyes, silent until now, interrupted. "Does this 'new spirituality' apply to your own house as well? Jesus said to remove the log from your own eye before pointing out the speck in another's. Mr. Sinclair, is your spiritual house in order?"

Tobias stared at the gaunt, middle-aged man. "What do you mean?"

"How can you preach spiritual truth when your own life raises questions? It's common knowledge your house needs correction."

"What are you trying to say, Reverend?" Tobias asked, irritation rising.

"Isn't it true your son is a practicing homosexual?"

Tobias's irritation turned to anger. The minister was trying to discredit him, his son, and the New Science with personal attacks. Tobias hadn't considered that some would feel so threatened they'd resort to smear tactics. He stayed calm.

"Everyone has gay people in their families. What does that have to do with the New Science or spirituality?"

"It is an unnatural sin," said the minister.

Tobias knew he had to defend his son. Though David's sexuality had contributed to their estrangement, Tobias had never rejected him. Their distance stemmed from Tobias's guilt—his absence during David's youth, his grief after Sharon's death, and his retreat into writing. David had stepped up, caring for his grandmother while Tobias remained emotionally unavailable. Tobias had loved his son unconditionally, but had failed to show it. He remembered David's silent stare at Sharon's funeral—an unspoken question of whether the wrong parent had died.

Now, Tobias's fatherly instincts surged.

"The New Science teaches us to view ourselves and our world objectively. Only then can we draw conclusions."

"Mr. Sinclair, you've probably heard 'God created Adam and Eve, not Adam and Steve.'"

Tobias didn't miss a beat. "If homosexuality is unnatural, how do you explain gay animals? Every species on Earth has a 10–15% homosexual population—not just mammals, but birds, reptiles, amphibians, fish, and insects."

The minister's smug expression turned irate. He had no answer.

Tobias continued, "And that 'Adam and Steve' line isn't in the Bible. But I'll tell you what is. In Matthew 19:12, Jesus said, 'For there are different reasons why men cannot marry: some, because they were born that way; others, because men made them that way; and others do not marry for the sake of the Kingdom of heaven. Let him who can accept this teaching do so.'"

"Sinclair, you're overstepping your authority," the minister warned.

"What you mean is that the New Science is stepping on your authority," Tobias replied. "And speaking of authority—you had no right to bring my son into this. The program is over. I'd appreciate it if you focused on the objective facts. Smear campaigns are beneath you."

Tobias stood and left the table.

The theologians were stunned. They filed out of the studio in silence—undefeated, yet without victory.

—

After the broadcast, Tobias was still steaming. He had promised to accompany Jimmy to the hospital to help bring Yolanda and Grace home. Mill went home in a cab. None of them expected the flood of reactions—emails, letters, and comments—some supporting Tobias, others excoriating him.

At the hospital, a middle-aged Latina woman approached Tobias as he waited for the elevator. She took his hand and kissed it.

"I've waited all my life to hear the things you said," she whispered.

Tobias was startled but gracious. He thanked her, though he didn't fully understand the depth of her response.

Later, Tobias brought Jimmy's car to the hospital entrance and waited in the driver's seat. He watched the lobby for Jimmy, Yolanda, and Grace to emerge.

Unbeknownst to him, a husky man in his late thirties with close-cropped red hair was approaching from behind. Tobias was unaware of the man as he watched the hospital lobby for Jimmy, Yolanda, and Grace to emerge.

As the elevator doors opened, the hospital attendant pushed Yolanda's wheelchair toward the exit and circular driveway. Jimmy walked attentively behind them, carrying Yolanda's small suitcase, a bouquet of flowers, and balloons celebrating Grace's arrival. Yolanda held Grace gently in her arms, radiant as a new mother, seated almost regally in her wheelchair.

As Tobias gazed at the sight of Jimmy and his new family, the redheaded man leaned toward Tobias through the open car window. In a low growl, he said, "You'd better be careful how you quote the Bible, Sinclair."

Tobias turned toward the grimacing face. Before the man could raise his clenched fist, Jimmy dropped the suitcase and flowers and darted to the car, placing himself between Tobias and the man. He pushed the man back.

"Too close, man! Move on!" Jimmy said, as Tobias slid to the passenger side to open the door for Yolanda.

Yolanda asked, "What was that all about?"

Tobias stood beside the car and helped Yolanda and Grace inside. "I don't know," he said. "Just a fan with too much enthusiasm."

They drove to Jimmy and Yolanda's apartment in Harlem. After Grace was settled in her crib, Tobias bid the young family farewell and took a cab home to Brooklyn. He barely spoke during the ride, immersed in thought. A strange mix of exhilaration and fear overcame him. The theologians, Stokes's absence, and the red-haired man swirled in his mind. Was the New Science movement spiraling out of control?

As the cab turned onto his tree-lined street in brownstone Brooklyn, Tobias saw his son, David, pacing outside the apartment building. David resembled Tobias— tall, thin, and brown.

A look of worry crossed Tobias's face. "David! Is everything OK? How's Grandma?"

"She's OK. I heard the broadcast on my way to New York."

148

"You never told me you listened to my program. I didn't think you were interested."

"Not only am I interested, but a couple of my friends checked you out."

"And the verdict?"

"Pop, I was going to surprise you anyway when you couldn't make it to Philly. I didn't know you knew so much. I'm proud of you."

They half shook hands, half embraced, and entered the building. As they climbed the steps to Tobias's apartment, they continued talking.

"I'm sorry they brought up your private life during the broadcast," Tobias said.

"I'm not worried about that, Pop," David replied. "They only know because I don't hide who I am. When it comes to my life, no one tells me—I tell them. But, Pop..."

Inside the apartment, now shadowy and gloomy at night, Tobias turned on the lamp beside the sofa. They sat—David on the sofa, Tobias in the easy chair.

"Pop, I came because I had to see you for myself. After San Francisco, you left us out of the loop. I had to look you in the eyes. But tonight—I couldn't believe what you said on the program. How did you know all those things from the Bible and nature? All this time I was trying to explain myself to you, and instead, you explained it to the whole world!"

"You taught me well, David."

"Dad…"

Tobias grew thoughtful. "I mean it. Being your father made me think about things I'd never considered. Something strange has happened to me, and I don't know how long it'll last. I have knowledge I didn't have before the mugging."

"Things?"

"Not just science—religion, human nature. I even understand you better. I feel more compassion, especially for those close to me. I know I haven't been the best father. We haven't always seen eye to eye—"

"Don't worry about that, Pop."

"And I know we haven't been as close as we should've been. But now's the time to fix that."

"Pop, you defended me on that show. You said things I didn't know you understood."

"The funny thing is—I didn't know I understood them either."

They smiled and embraced—truly this time—knowing their bond had been strengthened. David, tired from the drive and the emotional release, fell asleep in the second bedroom. He knew he'd see his father in a new light from that moment on.

—

The next morning, Tobias and David returned to Philadelphia. Tobias visited his widowed mother, looking for signs of resentment over his absence. But Rebecca seemed happy to see him, behaving as if no time had passed. Her perception of time had softened in recent years.

"Tobias, when are you going to stop writing those books and go back to being a lawyer?" she asked bluntly, still annoyed he'd left his profession.

"In due time, Mother," he replied, as always.

After Tobias's father died, his sister Janice—now a social worker—remained at home, living in the apartment once occupied by their uncle Kevin. Years ago, Kevin and Tobias's father had a falling out over the house. Kevin moved to Baltimore and had little contact with the family. Tobias's brother Willie drifted south to Atlanta, escaping what he saw as the family's slow unraveling.

It was left to Janice and David to hold the fort. The house that had once been full of life now felt cold and lifeless. The neighborhood had aged, and it showed.

Tobias stayed in Philadelphia for three days. For once, he let the New Science movement grow at its own pace. He relaxed in familiar surroundings, though never fully at ease in the presence of family.

The next afternoon, Janice returned from work and came upstairs to check on their mother. Though she had no children from her failed marriage, she helped fill the void left by Sharon's death. She remained "Aunt Janice" to David, though everyone knew she had become much more than that.

Janice used her key to open her mother's door. "Hey, everybody!" she said as she kissed her mother and hugged her nephew. Tobias stood near the kitchen table, smiling broadly.

She stopped, paused, and took a step back, exaggerating her movements. "Uh-oh! Look what the cat dragged in! Hello, stranger!"

They both broke into disarming laughter, hugging each other warmly. "You said you were all right on the phone," Janice said, "but I'm glad I can see for myself. That foolish mugger couldn't crack that old hard head of yours! You know I would've been there if you'd let me come."

Tobias smiled. "Sister, you know I would've called you if I needed help. But Jimmy and Mill had it all under control."

"Oh yes, your buddy Mill," said Janice, mockingly jealous. "Are you her brother from another mother, or is she your sister from another mister?"

"Both!"

All four shared a laugh as Tobias and Janice rocked side to side in a warm embrace. Eventually, each family member returned to their tasks. David left on an errand, Rebecca settled into her favorite home-shopping channel, and Tobias remained in the kitchen with Janice.

When they were finally alone, they sat at the kitchen table. Tobias peeled an orange from the fruit bowl and began to fill her in.

He told Janice about the man who had approached his car and the woman who had kissed his hand.

"You don't want to rouse people up too much, Tobias," she said, her voice tinged with concern.

"You're right. Mill told me we've been getting a lot of opinionated feedback since the last program with the ministers."

"Oh really? What did they say?"

"Well, the letters are split—maybe fifty-fifty or sixty-forty. Some think I'm the greatest thing since sliced bread. Others think I'm the devil incarnate."

"Let's hope the gut-haters are in the minority. You know David went to New York when he heard your last show. He was afraid for you."

"Afraid?"

"He's been through a lot lately, trying to 'find himself.' He's handling it well, but he was worried you were putting yourself out there too much."

"Sis, you've been there for him and Mom. I know I should've been more present than just sending a check now and then. What's this about David worrying about me? I was worried about him when they brought up his personal life during the broadcast."

"Don't sell him short. He's known how to deal with people like that for a long time. He was afraid you didn't understand."

"But that's just it, Janice. Since the mugging, I think I know more than I should. I didn't know I could recite the Bible by chapter and verse. I didn't know I knew about evolution, biology, animals—God knows what else. The seizures have mostly gone, but the knowledge is still there."

"Well, we all knew you were always a brain."

"Maybe a brain, but not like this." Tobias changed the subject, afraid he'd slip and mention Stokes and the extraterrestrials. He wanted to forget about them. "Don't worry, Janice. I won't let my hot head rule."

"Whatever it is, you've struck a nerve. You've stirred people up."

"I'm only stirring what needed to be stirred."

"Sometimes a boiling pot still boils, even if it's stirred," she said, standing up. "Maybe you need to turn the fire down a little."

She left the kitchen to return to her apartment downstairs. Tobias finished his orange and remained seated, considering her words.

—

Tobias stayed in Philadelphia for a few more days, then took a train back to New York. Sitting by the window, he watched the suburban landscape roll by, feeling a calm he'd never known before. He had reached an epiphany.

The key to true contentment resided within himself—his ability to resolve differences with David. The New

Science had helped him understand his son better, and had made him more approachable as a father.

He was able to reconcile the mugging, placing it in proper perspective. Though traumatic, it had opened his eyes. Like a clap of thunder, he suddenly and fully forgave the mugger—feeling strangely grateful for the experience that had brought him here.

His insights deepened. He forgave everyone in his life—his ex-wife, his father—both of whom had hurt and abandoned him through death. His anger melted into peaceful reflection. He felt they had forgiven him too.

He forgave himself—for his missteps with David, his law career, the mugging, his family, and even the theologians. As the train pulled into Penn Station, Tobias felt truly liberated. A newfound peace permeated his soul, and he wanted to share it with the world.

It was a short trip—ninety miles each way—but it may as well have been nine thousand. Like Saul transformed into Saint Paul on the road to Damascus, Tobias saw a new kind of light and became a new person on the ride from Philadelphia to New York.

—

Jimmy called soon after Tobias returned to his apartment.

"Hey, TS! How was Philly? How was the family?"

"Everybody was OK. I need to go back more often."

"Getting homesick?"

"Which home?"

"Good point. Listen, a news reporter wants to interview you. I think he's a science writer. What should I say?"

"Jimmy, I need a breather. No more lectures. No more interviews… at least for now."

"Whatever you say, boss. But we can't hold back the tide of progress."

"What tide?"

"Well, since you went away, Mill and I have been fielding calls left and right. People are becoming more interested in what you have to say."

"What people, Jimmy?"

"Scientists, human-rights groups, political organizations, animal-rights groups, gay-rights groups, multicultural organizations, New Age conferences. You name it."

"What?"

"I'm telling you, TS, Mill and I have been overwhelmed. They want you to speak!"

Tobias sat down on his bed, trying to absorb what Jimmy was saying.

"I have a stack of letters here I'm going to show you," said Jimmy. "And your publisher called. Your last book hit the best-seller list this week. They want to reprint your last two books to meet demand."

Tobias grew pensive. "Jimmy, what do you make of all of this?"

"After walking off your own show, you're finally getting noticed."

For the first time, Tobias wasn't sure he wanted to be noticed. Maybe his floundering writing career had always been a bid for recognition, but now he felt trapped—like a sideshow exhibit, the man with seizures who spouted wisdom.

"You know, Jimmy, my trip back to Philly helped me put things in perspective," Tobias said. "Sometimes I still feel like running away from the spectators. Or maybe I should just embrace the whole thing."

"Well, what are you going to do?"

"I guess I'm going to embrace it," Tobias replied. "And go with the flow. What else can I do?"

This marked a new level of inspiration. Philadelphia had cleared his mind, giving him insight and focus. His thoughts gelled as he continued speaking.

"If we're going to use the New Science to help us survive as a species," he told Jimmy, "we need to introduce it in a practical way. We need to show people how to wipe the slate clean. We need a Day of Forgiveness."

"A day of forgiveness? But you've already talked about love and forgiveness in other lectures, TS."

"I don't mean forgiveness in a general, idealistic sense. I mean a designated day—universal forgiveness for any wrongs, past or present. A fresh start."

"Who forgives whom? And for what?"

"Anything and everything. Individuals, countries, ethnic groups, religions."

"Shouldn't there be apologies first?"

"No. Forgiveness should come first—straight from the heart."

"Shouldn't forgiveness be taught by preachers?"

"That's the point. Theologians talk about forgiveness, but they've never united to propose a universal act. The more I learn from the New Science, the more I see that the physical and spiritual are one. And the only way to reconcile them is through unconditional love and forgiveness."

"TS, people have called you naive. Won't this give them more reason?"

"They've already called me crazy. But in my craziness, I think I know what's true—and what's needed."

Jimmy hesitated. "You sound like this whole thing's gone to your head."

Tobias looked around his bare apartment and out the window. "I don't even know how my head feels anymore,

Jimmy. All I know is I need to get this task done. I need to get these thoughts out into the light."

"But—"

"But nothing, Jimmy. I don't need a shrink or a debate. I need your help to get the word out. We need a Day of Forgiveness. That's our new mantra. Let's tell Mill."

Tobias clicked off the phone, proud to have found a decisive way to channel his knowledge while honoring Stokes's warning to reveal only what was necessary. With new inspiration, Tobias, Mill, and Jimmy designed the promotion for the Day of Forgiveness. It became the theme of the New Science website and the topic of a new course at the New School of Truth.

—

Two weeks later, Tobias and Mill visited Jimmy and Yolanda for a change of pace. Their regular meetings at Tobias's apartment had grown less focused, with Tobias absorbed in the Day of Forgiveness.

Mill quipped, "I'm tired of looking at your four walls, Toby. Let's meet at Jimmy's—and we can see Grace, too, Grandpa."

"Maybe seeing the baby will inspire us to think of the future," Tobias said, calling Jimmy to ask if it was okay. Jimmy and Yolanda always welcomed visits from Tobias and Mill, subtly considering them the parents they never had.

On their way to Manhattan, Mill and Tobias stopped at a drugstore to buy a toy for Grace.

159

"You know," said Mill, "the kid always expects some kind of goody when she sees us."

"Well, you're spoiling her too, Grandma!" Tobias teased.

They arrived a few minutes late, not expecting dinner, but Yolanda had prepared spaghetti with clam sauce.

"You didn't have to go through any trouble," said Mill.

"Don't worry," Yolanda replied, gazing down at Grace, now a toddler playing with her new baby piano. "With this little one running me ragged, the only thing I ever have time to do is boil water and dump a jar of sauce in a pot."

"That's more than I can do, honey," said Mill, and the two women laughed.

After dinner, Tobias, Mill, and Jimmy sat at the kitchen table while Yolanda tended to Grace.

Jimmy began, "TS, we're talking about the Day of Forgiveness, and we're telling people they must forgive to save humanity. But shouldn't there be an actual day designated for it? When will it take place?"

"Well, Jimmy," Tobias said, "if we set a date, not everyone could comply. Some might be ill, traveling, unavailable. And once the date passes, would people stop feeling obligated to forgive? I think it should be open-ended. Let each person, group, or country choose their own day."

"Toby, that doesn't make much sense," said Mill. "With no set date, we're just spinning our wheels. We'd be no different from religious leaders who say the same thing."

Jimmy added playfully, "Maybe the deadline should be the end of the Mayan calendar. If we don't forgive, we're doomed anyway!"

Tobias replied with frustration, "I still don't think it should be just one day! But since we're brainstorming, let's try to create at least a few clouds."

Mill said, "How about a forgiveness week or month?"

"Yeah," said Jimmy. "Like Breast Cancer Awareness Month."

"No," Tobias said. "That would only make people 'aware' they should forgive. They could still put it off. The goal is a fresh start. Mill's right—we need a specific day to unify the task. But how?"

Yolanda called in from the kitchen, washing dishes. "Why don't you have the Day of Forgiveness on the same day once each year?"

"Yeah," said Jimmy. "Like on the Mayan day, December 21!"

Tobias nodded his head. "I know that you're joking a little, Jimmy, but I must say that I kind of like that idea."
Mill agreed. "Sure, we could have the Day of Forgiveness on December 21 every year."

Tobias added, "You know, many cultures and religions have used the time around the winter solstice as a time of renewal and fresh starts."

Mill said with a gleam in her eye, "Why not? It's the shortest day of the year. They had to do something to keep the sun from disappearing!"

Thus, from that point on, they all agreed that the Day of Forgiveness would be held on December 21 of every year.

The following Wednesday marked Tobias's first broadcast since his confrontation with the religious leaders.

"Now's as good a time as any to officially announce the Day of Forgiveness," he told Mill and Jimmy during their meeting the night before.

"I'm not taking callers or guests," Tobias said. "I just want to explain why this day matters—and why it's urgent."

"Just don't make it sound like a manifesto," Jimmy warned.

"But that's exactly what it is," Tobias replied with a wink. "A manifesto for peace."

On the evening of the live webcast, Tobias felt a strange anxiety. Would his words help or hurt the cause? Would his reputation recover—or collapse entirely? He even tried to reach Stokes for advice. The reply came in a brief text: *The decision is yours alone to make.*

Tobias sat alone at the studio table, somber and focused. Mill and Jimmy watched quietly as he adjusted the microphone. There was no audience—just the camera, the silence, and the weight of what he was about to say.

"Welcome to the New School of Truth," he began. "I'm Tobias Sinclair. Tonight, I won't be taking calls. I only ask that you listen. These words may affect us all—for the rest of our lives. I'll try not to preach, but that may be inevitable. Please keep an open, absorbent mind—and see me as your equal."

He took a deep breath and whispered, "Here goes."

"We are a species on the verge of needless self-destruction. We have the capacity to understand our place in the universe—our reason for being. We are so close. Every intelligent species must face a moment like this: a decision to evolve or to perish through strife, greed, and violence. It's the true test of sentience.

"The New Age will be radically different from the present one. Human nature, as it stands, cannot sustain seven billion people if we continue to hate and kill. Whether Romans in the first century or Iraqis in the twenty-first, we have not changed. We are still destroying one another. That makes us a failed species.

"The universe, governed by balance and the laws of physics, reflects our actions back to us. We pollute the planet, torture and execute our own, and ignore the sacred. Any species capable of hanging, electrocuting, beheading, or crucifying its own kind has not earned the compassion of the universe. And in the absence of compassion, the devil finds work.

"If we refuse to change—if we won't share the earth peacefully with each other and with the plants and animals—we will obliterate ourselves. After such destruction, small enclaves may survive, but not seven billion people divided by borders and ideologies. Maybe seventy thousand. Maybe a hundred million. But they'll be living in a new Stone Age.

"So how do we save ourselves? There is a way. It's deceptively simple—but it works.

"We must choose a day to stop, reflect, and reset. A day to pause and choose a better path. The New Science teaches us that time is a physical dimension, like length or width. We've reached a fork in the road. We can 'stop' time by choosing a new direction—and 'restart' it by walking that path.

"I call this day the Day of Forgiveness.

"We suggest December 21—the winter solstice, a time of renewal. It's also the symbolic end of the Mayan calendar. And with every end, there is a beginning. If these are the End Times, then let us usher in the Beginning Times.

"On the Day of Forgiveness, we choose what comes next. Feed the hungry. Clothe the naked. House the homeless. Heal the sick. Educate the masses. Use renewable energy. Stop fighting over borders, race, religion, and sexuality. Recognize that we live on one planet—and we must share it equally with each other and with all living beings.

"If we do nothing, our civilization will end. If we choose fear—selfishness, violence, bigotry—we will not survive. Fear is the opposite of love. It's a lower energy, a shorter wavelength. If love is green, fear is red. And if we act from fear, we work against love, against the universe, against God.

This is a pivotal moment in human history. The only way forward is love—consistent, courageous love. In our smallest decisions and our global choices. This is what the Day of Forgiveness is for.
It's as close as your mind. As simple as your actions.

Forgive yourselves. Forgive each other.

Join us in saving our species—and our planet."

Chapter 7: The Ripple Effect

Tobias turned off the microphone and leaned back in his chair. The studio was silent, save for the soft hum of the closing music. Mill and Jimmy watched from the control booth, neither speaking. They knew something had shifted—not just in Tobias, but in the world.

Within minutes, the inbox flooded. Emails, texts, voice messages. Some were euphoric, others furious. Many were simply stunned. The reactions were as varied as the senders—scientists, students, spiritual seekers, skeptics, and strangers. Some called Tobias a prophet. Others called him dangerous. But all agreed on one thing: something had happened.

He had struck a nerve.

Mill stayed late that night, sorting through the avalanche of messages. She read each one with the precision of a lawyer and the heart of a believer. By morning, she had made her decision.

"Toby," she said, walking into his apartment with a stack of printed emails, "I've officially closed my practice."

Tobias looked up, surprised. "You did?"

"I would only give up my career for a cause worth fighting for. This is more than worth it."

From that day forward, Mill became the full-time director of operations for the New School of Truth. She handled legal affairs, financial planning, and the growing web of partnerships and inquiries. Tobias continued to speak and teach, while Jimmy—now trained in security—managed logistics and kept a watchful eye on the movement's more unpredictable followers.

Though there were no credible threats, Tobias's message had begun to challenge the foundations of society. He didn't just promote the New Science—he questioned the order of things. And that made people nervous.

For the next several months, Tobias experienced no seizures. It was as if the act of sharing the Day of Forgiveness had released something inside him. He spoke with clarity and conviction, linking the New Science to world peace, and the message resonated. Crowds grew. Classes filled. Public television offered airtime. The school expanded.

Eventually, the New School of Truth evolved into the New Science University. It rivaled traditional institutions in size and scope. Online courses flourished. The Day of Forgiveness gained traction across continents. Tobias remained in his modest Brooklyn apartment, but his influence was anything but small.

And with influence came complexity.

Among the students were casual followers—those who knew just enough to sound enlightened at dinner parties. Others were deeply committed scholars, immersed in the curriculum. But there was a third group—zealots. Jimmy watched them closely. They weren't scientists or seekers. They were wanderers looking for something to believe in. For them, Tobias wasn't a teacher. He was a messiah.

Tobias tried to redirect their energy. He encouraged service, humility, and practical action. But many remained restless. The Day of Forgiveness became their obsession— a symbol of salvation, a countdown to transformation.

The movement had become a mirror of the 1960s. Just as hippies once reshaped culture, the followers of the New Science began to reshape conversation. "Are you a Truther?" became a common question—equal parts identity and invitation.

Tobias laughed when Jimmy first used the term. "How does it feel to be the first Truther?"

Jimmy grinned. "You mean before that bump on your head, there were no Truthers!"

They could joke now. Time had softened the trauma. Tobias spoke openly about the mugging, even referencing it in lectures. "I forgave him long before he ever apologized," he told one student. "Without the burden of anger, I'm free. He's the one still bound."

But not all was light and laughter. The movement was growing. So was the tension.

And somewhere, in the shadows, a new force was beginning to stir.

Tobias had spoken of forgiveness. Now he would live it.

A few weeks after the broadcast, he boarded a flight to San Francisco. The city where it all began. The cool Pacific breeze greeted him like a whisper from the past. It had been over a year since the mugging—since the seizures, the revelations, the broadcasts, and the birth of the Day of Forgiveness. He returned not as a victim, but as a messenger.

The man who had attacked him was now serving a life sentence without parole. Tobias had followed the case quietly. The mugger—whose name had only recently emerged—had fatally injured another man in a similar assault just weeks after Tobias's own. The trial had been swift. The sentence severe. Tobias had never thought openly about his mugger's fate. Until now.

He took a cab to the city's central detention facility. The prison was stark and gray, perched like a fortress on the edge of the city. Tobias walked through the metal detectors, signed the visitor log, and waited in a sterile room with plastic chairs and a thick pane of glass separating him from the inmates.

The man was led in by a guard. He was older now, worn, his black hair faded and thinning. He looked at Tobias with a mixture of confusion and recognition.

"You're the guy I hit," he said flatly.

Tobias nodded. "Yes. I'm Tobias Sinclair."

The man sat down, his eyes wary. "Why are you here?"

"I came to forgive you."

The man blinked. "Forgive me?"

"Yes. You changed my life. Not in the way you intended, but in a way that matters. I don't condone what you did. I don't excuse it. But I understand now that pain can be a doorway. You opened mine."

The man looked away. "I didn't mean to change your life. I was just angry. High. Broke. I didn't care."

"I know," said Tobias. "But I do. And I believe that forgiveness is the only way forward—for me, for you, for all of us."

The man's eyes welled up, but he didn't speak.

Tobias continued, "You're part of my story now. And I needed to come here to say that I release you. Not from your sentence, but from my anger. I release myself, too."

The silence between them was heavy, but not hostile. It was the silence of two men standing at the edge of something larger than themselves.

As Tobias stood to leave, the man said quietly, "No one's ever forgiven me before."

Tobias turned back. "Then let this be your first Day of Forgiveness."

Outside the prison, the sun was beginning to set over the bay. Tobias walked slowly, feeling the weight of the moment settle into his bones. He had come full circle—not to erase the past, but to honor it. The mugger had taken something from him, but he had also given him something Tobias never expected: a new beginning.

And now, Tobias was ready to share that beginning with the world.

Back in New York, with the Day of Forgiveness movement in full swing, Tobias received a call on his private cell phone—a number known only to Jimmy, Mill, and close family.

It was Stokes.

"We need to meet again, Mr. Sinclair," he said. "We must discuss your growing fame. I'm sure you have questions about how to best use it."

Tobias hadn't thought of Stokes in months. He had tried to dismiss their first encounter as the ramblings of a disturbed man. But now, hearing that voice again, something stirred.

"When I tried to contact you for advice," Tobias said, "you told me to use my best judgment. You left me flapping in the breeze. Now you want to give me advice again? What gives?"

"You've been doing fine, Mr. Sinclair. Until now, there was no need to interfere. You handled the New Science well, and you were discreet. Your Day of Forgiveness was well received. But now you're becoming well-known. I think it's time you knew more."

Tobias hesitated, then nodded. "Should we meet tonight?"

"The sooner, the better."

It was nearly ten o'clock. The streets were quiet. Within the hour, Stokes rang the buzzer and was let into Tobias's apartment. Tobias opened the door, suddenly unsure about letting him in.

Stokes began speaking without greeting. "I'm sorry if I conveyed urgency, but things are changing rapidly."

"What things?"

"As you know, human communication is constantly monitored by my community. We observe television, radio, satellite, Internet, and phone transmissions."

"In other words, the extraterrestrials are bugging us," Tobias said, trying to mask his cynicism. He motioned for Stokes to sit while he stood by the window.

"You could put it that way. But we've noticed a pattern that concerns us."

"I'm aware of the security risks. My assistant has things under control. And I'm not running for office."

"This isn't about politics or security," Stokes said. "It's about the public's response to your campaign. There's a trend that may impact your future—and humanity's."

"A trend?"

"Yes. Some now see you not as a teacher or scientist, but as a religious figure. They've formed groups and websites. They call you the Black Messiah, the Helper of the End Times, the Savior from the Awful Horror Jesus mentioned in the Bible."

"What?"

"Not just average people. Even religious leaders are concerned. Some want to exalt you. Others want to eliminate you."

A chill ran through Tobias. He sat down. "I'm just a guy who got hit on the head and saw the light. I haven't performed any miracles."

"You have, Mr. Sinclair. The miracle was the knowledge you shared. You've challenged the foundations of religion, government, science, and society. We've never seen anything like this."

Tobias felt fear creeping in—not of Stokes, but of human nature. The implications of the New Science were dawning on him. "Maybe I shouldn't have met with the theologians. Maybe I should've left forgiveness alone. I'm no messiah. I don't want this."

"Before you make any rash decisions," Stokes said, standing, "I need to show you something. I know it's late, but this is the best time."

Tobias stood too. Somewhere between fear and bewilderment, he wanted answers. He grabbed his jacket and followed Stokes out the door.

Stokes's car was parked outside. Tobias brought his phone, just in case Jimmy needed to reach him. They drove out of Brooklyn, through Manhattan, and across the George Washington Bridge. Northward into upstate New York. The city lights faded. The road grew darker. Lonelier.

After an hour of silence, broken only by the radio, Stokes spoke.

"Mr. Sinclair, I'm honored you trusted me."

Tobias looked out the window. "My assistant says I trust people too much. But I can see you're trying to help. Still, your story was hard to digest. It's not every day I meet someone from outer space."

Stokes smiled faintly. "I didn't expect you to believe me right away. You know a lot from our first meeting. It must've sounded strange—that I wasn't raised on Earth."

"Do you have a family?"

"I'm not married. I have a sister. Our parents raised us among other abductees and extraterrestrials. It's funny, though."

"What's funny about that?"

"Funny that while Earth's people are unaware of us, I always felt invisible. Like an outsider looking in. My sister and I wondered what it would've been like to grow up on Earth. But we were stuck in our 'special' circumstances."

Tobias turned to him. "Are there many like you?"

"Not many. Seven of us are on the current ship monitoring Earth—three humans, four extraterrestrials. A few dozen humans live in the extraterrestrial society. Some stay on colonized planets. Some, like me, work with them to monitor Earth's progress. It's my way of giving back."

"Giving back?" Tobias asked. "To people who never gave anything to you?"

Stokes paused. "I wanted to learn about my roots. To understand my species and the planet my parents were taken from long ago."

"How long ago?"

Stokes hesitated. "This will be the first fact that may shake your belief system."

"Go on," Tobias said. "At this point, nothing will surprise me."

"My parents were abducted over four hundred and fifty years ago. My father in 1503. My mother in 1547."

Stokes looked over at Tobias.

"I am three hundred and twenty-eight years old."

Tobias stared at Stokes in disbelief. He looked like a man in his forties—dark hair, youthful face, calm demeanor. Was this man completely insane? Or was Tobias himself trapped in a relentless dream?

"Don't be afraid, Mr. Sinclair," said Stokes, seemingly reading his thoughts. "I guess you can be surprised after all. Extraterrestrial technology has enabled lifespans far beyond what nature allows. Do you remember the biblical giants? The 'sons of God' and 'daughters of men'? Methuselah?"

"Yes, of course," Tobias replied, trying not to sound shaken.

"Well, the extraterrestrials had a hand in that. And they still do—extending their own lives and those of the humans in their community."

They drove in silence for another half hour. Tobias tried to absorb what he'd heard.

"We're almost there," Stokes said.

"Where is there?"

They turned off the highway onto a narrow country road. The darkness thickened. Only the headlights cut through the void.

Then, without warning, the car's lights were joined by another glow—soft, multicolored, hovering above a clearing in the woods.

A spacecraft.

They pulled to the edge of the clearing. Tobias stared, mesmerized.

"Please don't be afraid," said Stokes. "You know a great deal already. I'd like to take you on board to meet the team. The stories you've heard—abductions, experiments—were mostly true. But those people were afraid. They didn't understand. They were examined, tagged, released."

"Like animals on a preserve," Tobias murmured, transfixed by the ship's beauty.

"Yes. But this is different. You're aware. You have a choice."

"There's just one thing," Stokes added. "Seeing extraterrestrials for the first time can be… disconcerting. Try to remember—they're thinking, caring, intelligent beings. Just like us."

"Maybe better than us," Tobias said.

"You said it," Stokes smiled.

The ship hovered silently, twenty feet off the ground. A door opened beneath it, releasing a ramp. Tobias felt a strange calm. He was being given a choice—and that made all the difference.

"I'm ready when you are," he said.

They walked up the ramp together.

Inside, the curved walls glowed softly. The space was larger than expected. Four figures stood at the top of the steps: two humans, one extraterrestrial, and a hybrid woman.

The humans—Richard and Beatrice—appeared to be of mixed ethnicities. The extraterrestrial was reptilian, hairless, under five feet tall, with smooth gray-green skin and large dark eyes. The hybrid woman, Serena, had piercing eyes and thin, dark hair. Two other extraterrestrials sat farther inside, operating the craft.

"Welcome," said Beatrice. She motioned to the others. "This is Richard. And this is Serena."

"Hello," Tobias said, awestruck.

"My name is Goren," said the extraterrestrial. His mouth never moved.

"I'm sure you have questions," Richard said. "But I trust Stokes has filled you in. We can't get him to shut up either."

They laughed. Tobias noticed Goren's laughter wasn't audible—it was felt, almost telepathic.

"We've asked you here," said Serena, both aloud and telepathically, "because you're about to play a pivotal role in human history."

Goren added, "Your work will help humanity transition from tribalism to universality. But you need to understand true human history—and what's at stake."

Tobias was given a brief tour, then led to a small conference room. Serena and Richard returned to their stations. Stokes, Beatrice, and Goren joined Tobias around an oval white table. A teakettle sat in the center, surrounded by cups and saucers.

They poured spearmint tea. Tobias sipped, strangely comforted by the ritual.

"We're glad you came," said Beatrice. "Stokes speaks highly of you."

Goren leaned forward. "Your New Science teachings are closer to reality than you know. You've stumbled onto the truth of the universe. The question is—what will you do with it? Hide it? Exploit it? Use it to educate and unify?"

"How can I educate humanity," Tobias asked, "when I know so little?"

"That's why we invited you," said Stokes. "We want to share the history of humanity—so you can decide how best to use what you've learned. The choice is yours."

"I see," said Tobias with new resolve. "Well, let's get started."

Stokes continued, "You were correct during your lectures, Mr. Sinclair, when you told your audience that we humans have had technology in the past that was more advanced than what we have today. We've had aircrafts before, as well as telephones and computers. But every time we reached a certain level of sophistication, we would end up destroying ourselves through warfare, divisions, and conflicts. It is true that we bombed ourselves back into the Stone Age each time and have had to start all over again. Maybe this time will be different, but when we monitor today's news of wars and conflicts, it seems that humans are, again, headed along the same path of self-destruction."

The lights dimmed in the room, and Tobias was shown what seemed to be remarkable recordings of pyramids and other stone structures being built by humans and extraterrestrials in ancient times, as well as the construction of the land drawings on the open plains of Nazca, Peru, the building of the statues on Easter Island, and the construction of Stonehenge, Machu Picchu, and other sites. Tobias was taught mostly by Goren, who telepathically informed him of historical facts. He now understood how some ancient maps were drawn of the New World, Antarctica, and other landmasses long before they were discovered in modern times. He was also informed of the truth behind the Dogon people of Africa who had known about the rings of Saturn and the moons of Jupiter and that the Dog Star, Sirius, was a twin star long before any of these observations were discovered in modern times with modern telescopes. Tobias was also taught the truth behind the book of Ezekiel, which seemed to describe an encounter with a UFO, and the list went on and on. Goren said, "The evidence was right under humanity's collective nose, but people chose to ignore it."

Tobias asked, "What happened to cause things to go so wrong? Why did these past civilizations disappear? With such a rich history, why haven't we advanced any further than we have up to this point?"

"The answer is in your own religious books," answered Goren. "Especially the story of the Tower of Babel in the book of Genesis. You may recall that, at one time, the people of the earth shared one language and culture, but God scattered them across the earth. People could no longer communicate with each other because each group developed its own language. This is exactly what happened; the extraterrestrial culture deserted humans to allow them to evolve on their own, resulting in the sudden loss of advanced technology. This resulted in the migration of humans across the globe, and over time they were no longer able to communicate with one another. New languages, religions, cultures, and countries subsequently developed. Yet the myth of a Great Flood wiping out civilization and forcing people to start over again is seen in many cultures and has remained an important part of your prehistory."

"Why did the extraterrestrial culture end?" asked Tobias.

"The culture did not end," said Beatrice, slightly annoyed. "We still have what you call 'the extraterrestrial culture.' We live on a number of planets and satellites. The culture consists of several species of sentient beings, including some humans. The extraterrestrial culture never ended. What indeed ended was the helping hand that the extraterrestrials had extended to the humans of the earth."

Goren interrupted, "Let's give you a crash course in the history of the interactions between extraterrestrials and humans."

"OK," said Tobias, taking a sip of his tea.

Stokes started the discussion. "The extraterrestrial community has been around for a long time, and human contact with their culture occurred from forty thousand years ago until about twenty thousand years ago. During that period, they helped humanity to advance in scientific knowledge and in the construction of the stone pyramids and buildings that you saw in the videos. The reason the extraterrestrials stopped interacting with humans was that we humans had become increasingly arrogant and had abused our privileged status of having the knowledge of the universe at our fingertips. We began to abuse our relationship with the universe, with the planet, with the extraterrestrials, and with each other. We began to have a negative impact on the natural environment, just as the present-day humans of the earth are polluting our lands, sea, and air.

"After the extraterrestrials left the humans of the earth to develop on our own, we still had plenty of time, tens of thousands of years, to develop agriculture, civilization, and technology. We had enough time to develop societies, some even more advanced than our present-day culture. Instead, we polluted the earth and fought one another over the limited resources, coming close to destroying our planet. Civilizations were destroyed time and time again, and each cycle correlated well with the long cycles in the Mayan calendar lasting for thousands of years."

Goren added, "Yet the main events that had shaped the development of humans were based on conditions that occurred in the environment, not on any intervention by my species. You were right, Mr. Sinclair, when you explained to your audience the myths across many cultures and religions that speak of civilization being nearly wiped out by a deluge, or Great Flood, that may have molded and influenced the development of humanity."

"The Great Flood shaping humankind? Is that what you're saying?" asked Tobias.

"Is that so far-fetched?" asked Beatrice. "It sort of questions your own beliefs, doesn't it? You know, human archaeologists have found water marks on the Sphinx."

"On the Sphinx? In the Sahara?"

"Yes," she replied. "The Sahara wasn't always a desert. And the Sphinx is a lot older than you may think."

"I'm sorry to say this, Mr. Sinclair," added Goren, "but the Great Cleansing as prophesized by the Hopi and other people may become the next Great Flood for humanity. Even if humans are able to attain the true knowledge of the New Science and understand who they are as a species, it may not be sufficient to provide the necessary wisdom to save humanity and the planet from disaster. The humans of the earth seem to turn their backs on the evidence and have always been difficult to teach."

Tobias lamented, "So then I've just been wasting my time over the past few years trying to teach the New Science. It was all for nothing."

"I wouldn't say that," assured Stokes. "We just want you to know how frustrating it can be to work with our human species, especially when they're unenlightened. The extraterrestrials abandoned us out of sheer frustration."

Beatrice added, "Yet back then, they abandoned humans not only because we had polluted the physical earth but also because we had polluted the spiritual earth, the energy from which our spirits come. We had become extremely corrupt and were acting no differently than we do today, yet it was much worse back then because we should have known better. We were supposedly enlightened. This made our crime many times as worse than today because it involved the abuse of the knowledge of the universe. We willfully abused the New Science."

Goren added, "My species decided to leave your human ancestors alone to enable them to forget all that we had taught them. They knew that human nature is such that the knowledge would eventually be lost and that humans would revert back to a new dark age and be unable to preserve the teachings, or anything else, for thousands of years."

"The Tower of Babel," said Tobias.

"Indeed," continued Stokes. "Our human ancestors essentially regressed back to the Stone Age. We lost most of the knowledge and technology for the one thousand to three thousand years after the extraterrestrials left. For the next ten thousand years or so—that is, from 17,000 to 7000 BC—we remained hunter-gatherers and later redeveloped agriculture. Today, even the oldest continuous cultures and written languages only go back four thousand or five thousand years—that is, back to around 3000 BC."

"Well, don't we have some idea of the historical events that happened since that time through written accounts and oral history?" asked Tobias.

"Yes, from the ancient Egyptians onward," answered Goren. "But human history is still full of unanswered questions, and there are a number of gaps and mysteries. Think of the extraterrestrials as a group of missionaries. Their mission is to find and aid any species that is intelligent enough to understand the concepts of God and the universe but may be held back by some anomaly in its evolution or development. I joined the mission after my closest friend from school was killed in the UFO crash in Roswell, New Mexico, in 1947. His corpse was one of the alien bodies that was recovered by human officials. I was inspired to carry on his work by volunteering to serve in this surveillance project to observe the humans of the earth. My goal was to continue his study of the anomaly that had prevented the advancement of the human species."

"What anomaly is that?" asked Tobias.

"The human anomaly is the persistence of an aggressive and territorial nature despite having advanced intelligence," replied Goren. "This seems to lead to all of humanity's problems."

Stokes concluded, "The extraterrestrials had to leave us—to isolate us—so we could forget the time long ago when we had the power to understand who we really were. For the past twenty thousand years, they've stood by, monitoring our development. Mr. Sinclair, if humanity can rediscover the true nature of the universe on its own, we will have earned the privilege to rejoin the network of sentient species. But if we destroy ourselves before reaching that understanding, then that is our fate. And it will be our fault—because we are smart enough to recognize the danger, yet unwilling to act.

"When humanity reaches a consensus—when we understand our evolution and our place in the cosmos—the extraterrestrials may once again share their knowledge. Their hands-off approach will end. Our isolation will be over. We will no longer feel alone in the universe. The Mayan, Gregorian, Chinese, Hebrew, and other calendars will become obsolete. A new dawn will emerge."

Tobias nodded, though he felt increasingly overwhelmed.

Goren stepped closer, his large, dark eyes locking onto Tobias. "Mr. Sinclair, you can now see the role you may play in this."

"What role?"

"You are in a position to help humanity recognize the true nature of the universe—and to reach consensus. You can help usher in the Age of Aquarius."

Tobias was speechless. He stared at Stokes, Beatrice, and Goren as if each had grown five heads.

Beatrice softened her tone. "We're not trying to put words in your mouth or force you into anything. But you needed to know what's at stake."

Goren added, "Human life could be so much better. You could become creatures of reason—guided by intellect, not emotion or aggression. My species struggled with this same dilemma millions of years ago."

Tobias gathered his courage. "What is your species? Where do you come from?"

Goren, speaking mostly telepathically, with his small mouth barely moving, replied, "You've asked the right question. I know you've imagined me as coming from some distant planet. You've wondered why my species cares so deeply about humanity. And you've wondered about Serena, our hybrid team member."

"Yes."

"Well, Mr. Sinclair, the truth is—what you and most of humanity think of as 'creatures from outer space' are nothing of the kind."

"What do you mean?"

"It may surprise you to learn that my species are Earthlings too," said Goren, pausing for effect. "Yes, Mr. Sinclair—I am of the Earth."

Tobias scanned Goren from head to toe. "Earthlings?"

"Yes," Goren said, sensing Tobias's rising fear. "Don't worry—we're not human. You're not going to evolve into me." Beatrice and Stokes smiled knowingly.

"I'm not from another planet," Goren continued. "I am a member of a species of dinosaur that evolved on Earth tens of millions of years ago."

"Dinosaur?"

"You look surprised. But there are descendants of dinosaurs all around you. You call them birds."

Tobias tried to process it. "But weren't the dinosaurs wiped out by a meteor sixty-five million years ago?"

"Yes," Goren said. "But birds survived by flying to safety. My ancestors survived through intelligence and protection. Like humans, we were tree-dwelling dinosaurs with opposable thumbs. We had an aquatic phase that expanded our brains. By the time of the meteor crash, we had underground shelters, underwater habitats, and access to space stations. Earth is our home—just as much as it is yours. We have a vested interest in its future."

"Such as humans?"

"Such as humans, dolphins, whales, crows, and bonobos," Goren said. "We don't mean to lump humans with animals—but we are all animals. Humans are special. You understand the universe. You manipulate the environment with opposable thumbs. The challenge is to do so wisely—spiritually. We care deeply about your success. We don't want to see you destroy our shared home."

Beatrice added, "Goren's species call themselves the Naku. They believe it's against the natural flow of the universe to interfere too directly. It would violate their spiritual beliefs to 'play God.' Still, they tried to guide humanity in the past. It didn't work."

"Yet Serena is proof of what we achieved," said Goren. "She is a hybrid of our two species—a link to our common Earth origin. Though conceived artificially, her existence proves our shared genetic evolution."

Tobias sat in stunned silence. "Why me? Why do you want me to tell everyone?"

Stokes placed a hand on Tobias's shoulder. "Maybe we've given you too much. Maybe we went too far. I

186

apologize if we overwhelmed you. We don't expect you to usher in the Age of Aquarius alone. But we believe you can help people adjust to the truth. Just be careful of those who would place you on a pedestal."

"You don't have to worry about that," Tobias said, his voice low and hoarse. "But this is a tall order."

Beatrice smiled. "Mr. Sinclair, this is far from an order. The choices are yours. We just wanted you to understand how important your work may be."

Goren added, "We'll continue monitoring global communications about the New Science and about you. If there's cause for concern, we'll be in touch. Our goal tonight was simply to inform you—and help you make thoughtful, intelligent decisions."

Stokes nudged him. "Ready to go home?"

Tobias gave a sheepish grin. "Can't I stay here with you guys?"

They all smiled as Tobias and Stokes descended the ramp and returned to the car. The spacecraft's door slid closed, and the ship rose silently into the sky—bearing witness to a turning point in Tobias's life.

Chapter 8: Creatures of Reason

Stokes and Tobias returned to Brooklyn in silence. Tobias sat stunned, staring out the passenger-side window as the solid yellow and broken white lines on the asphalt stretched into the night like quiet guides. When Stokes flicked on the high beams, the lines sharpened—straight as arrows, reaching toward home.

Crossing the Brooklyn Bridge, Tobias remained deep in thought, unable to fully grasp what he had just experienced. As they turned onto his familiar street and stopped in front of his building, Stokes said, "This is the first time we've allowed a human of Earth to see what you've seen—and let him go."

"Thanks, I think," Tobias replied, managing a faint joke now that he was back in his own territory.

"I know we've given you a lot to digest," Stokes said gently. "We hope your goals and decisions will have new clarity."

"Clarity? No. Understanding? Maybe," Tobias said as he stepped out of the car. "Or at least I'm working on it."

He closed the door, then added with a smirk, "By the way, nice car. How do you afford a Mercedes on a professor's salary?"

"I used the spaceship as collateral, Mr. Sinclair."

They shared a muted laugh, like old friends. As Stokes drove off, he called out, "Call me if you need me."

It was nearly dawn. Tobias returned home to find sunlight streaming through his windows and starlings announcing the new day. He rarely saw his apartment in this light. He sank into his easy chair, closed his eyes, and let the sun dance across his face. Too exhausted to be frightened, he remained immersed in thought.

He made a quiet decision: he would not, and could not, tell Mill, Jimmy, or anyone else about his trip with Stokes. He still questioned whether it had truly happened. Had he really been aboard a spacecraft? He knew now that Stokes had told the truth, but he also knew how others would react. "Do I really care what they think?" he asked himself. At that moment, he resolved to walk the path alone—but he would use his new knowledge to guide the school.

He fell asleep in the chair. The day continued without him.

—

In the months that followed, Tobias exhibited renewed motivation. He poured his spirit into the New Science University, insisting that every class reflect the core principle: that humans can use objective observation, tempered by love and forgiveness, to study any subject. The New Science fused empirical inquiry with karma, chi, chakras, and the positive energies of the universe—enhancing meaning across disciplines.

Enrollment surged. Tobias expanded the curriculum through forums, online chats, and new courses in physics, mathematics, astronomy, sociology, biology, and chemistry—all taught through the lens of the New Science. The university didn't rival traditional science—it complemented it. Other institutions began to adopt the model, blending conventional and New Science philosophies.

During one meeting, Mill asked, "Doesn't it bother you that these other schools are stealing our stuff? They're using the New Science to advance their own careers."

Tobias replied, "If they use it positively, it helps our cause too."

With the Day of Forgiveness campaign in full swing, Tobias became a new kind of leader. Scientists and theologians sought him out to discuss physics, cosmology, and God—topics that kept surfacing in light of the movement.

But after the trip with Stokes, Tobias grew increasingly reclusive. He often told Jimmy, "I'll be all right," before disappearing down subway steps. He focused solely on the New Science and the Day of Forgiveness, distancing himself from Jimmy, Yolanda, Mill, and even his family.

One evening, Jimmy invited Tobias over for dinner after a webcast. Even Tobias knew he needed a break. He looked forward to spending time with Jimmy, Yolanda, and Grace. He realized they'd invited him without Mill because they were worried.

Grace was now a year and a half old—curious, joyful, radiant. Seeing her reminded Tobias of his own son, of his responsibilities as a father. After his ex-wife's accident, he had learned to hide his loneliness. He tried to forget what David was like as a baby, hoping to suppress the feelings of fatherly nurturance. But with Grace, he played the role of Grandpa just fine. For a few hours, a void was filled.

That night, Tobias returned home feeling relaxed and joyful—satisfied by a home-cooked meal and the company of an innocent child.

Then he noticed a message on his voicemail.

"Mr. Sinclair, I don't know whether you remember me, but this is Dr. Patel. I treated you early last year in San Francisco. Please call me back. I have something I'd like to discuss with you."

Tobias smiled, recalling the warm rapport they'd shared. Her voice reminded him of the chaos of his recovery—and how much had changed since. It felt like a lifetime ago.

He jotted down the number and called her immediately.

"It's good to hear from you," he said.

"Thank you for calling back, Mr. Sinclair. I hope you're well. I haven't read anything about any new seizures."

"It's been a while. I've been a good little boy," he said playfully.

"I had to phone you," Dr. Patel said, her voice unusually excited. "I thought you should be among the first to know."

"Know what?"

"Well," she said, shifting to a more professional tone, "since your discharge, I've followed your work. I've read your books. I even took several New Science courses online. A few months ago, I decided to apply what I learned to my medical research."

"I didn't know you were doing research. Seizures?"

"No. I study HIV and AIDS."

"Doc, you're remarkable."

"That's just it," she replied. "What's remarkable isn't me—or even the research. It's the New Science."

Tobias blinked. "The New Science?"

"Yes. When I applied it to the AIDS process, a whole new perspective opened up. Your classes taught me that our universe is an electron in a carbon atom—and that life is a subtle phase of carbon within that electron universe. When I viewed the virus and the immune system as units of this life phase, with carbon atoms interacting, the disease made more sense. Nothing changed in how AIDS works. What changed was how we see it. The carbon of the virus's RNA interacts with the carbon in the host cell's chromosomes, triggering protein production that helps the virus reproduce."

"A different perspective?"

"Yes," Dr. Patel replied. "And a different treatment—and cure. Our preliminary studies are promising. We're targeting the proteins produced by infected cells that allow the virus to replicate. It's clear there's a balance between the virus and the cell's chromosomes—a balance we may be able to disrupt with medicines and vaccines. I felt you should be the first to know: your work in the New Science may save millions of lives, Mr. Sinclair."

"Dr. Patel, I'm not a doctor," Tobias said, now accustomed to surprises. "But I've learned that the New Science doesn't change science—it changes our perspective. What did you see when you applied it?"

"The New Science helped us see HIV and the immune system differently. Immunity and the virus are two sides of the same coin—yin and yang. The cure must be part of that balance."

"You're saying the New Science can be used to cure diseases?"

"That's exactly what I'm saying. And the same approach could apply to cancer, diabetes, autoimmune disorders, spinal injuries, brain trauma—a host of conditions."

Tobias was speechless. He already knew the New Science posed a threat to the established order—politicians, theologians, institutions. Redefining forgiveness had unsettled the religious world. Now, redefining healing would shake the medical establishment.

"Dr. Patel, I guess we've opened a real can of worms," he said, grasping the enormity of it.

"I just thought you should know how we're using the New Science to help people. Thank you, Mr. Sinclair."

"The thanks belong to the universe," Tobias said solemnly.

He ended the call with a strange feeling—like he should be thanking her, not the other way around.

—

Tobias found himself torn by the New Science, which was reshaping the very identity he had tried to build. Was he a lawyer, a writer, a preacher, a philosopher, a scientist? He no longer cared. The chips had fallen. He wouldn't try to pick them up.

Dr. Patel's research was published soon after their conversation, and her team became world-renowned. She always cited the New Science—and Tobias Sinclair—as the source. Her work had particular impact in India and the developing world, where inexpensive treatments were now within reach. The New Science University gained credibility. The movement gained momentum.

But Tobias grew increasingly despondent. He withdrew further into himself, even as he remained busy—lecturing, broadcasting, answering questions. He avoided socializing with Mill and Jimmy, though he saw them daily at work. They sensed the change and gave him space. He visited his family in Philadelphia only occasionally. Despite being surrounded by people, he was profoundly alone.

He carried himself as if the New Science had placed the weight of the world on his shoulders. He continued to promote the Day of Forgiveness, though he couldn't share the source of his motivation—or his knowledge of Stokes and the extraterrestrials. He didn't know where it would lead. But he knew the goal: the enlightenment of humanity, and his own growth.

Eventually, Tobias agreed to meet again with a mixed group of cosmologists, physicists, biologists, and other professionals. By now, the scientific community had begun to accept the New Science—not because it contradicted their work, but because it complemented it. They wanted clarity. They wanted to understand how it applied to their fields. Hostility had faded. Respect had grown.

Jimmy picked up Tobias at his apartment. They drove in silence from Brooklyn into Manhattan. Jimmy wasn't surprised—Tobias had been distant for months. Ever since the second meeting with Stokes, of which Jimmy knew nothing, Tobias spoke only of logistics and lectures.

This time, Jimmy broke the silence.

"You know, we're not going to the studio."

"Where are we going?" Tobias asked.

"A theater near Twenty-Third Street."

"A theater? Why?"

"Well, TS, you're in demand. We needed a bigger venue. It's been a couple of years since you met with the physicists. You remember what happened last time…"

"Yeah, Jimmy. I'd rather forget."

"I'm only mentioning it because I want to know if you're really up for this. Remember the theologians? People got weird when you talked about the Bible."

"Don't worry," Tobias said. "I won't mention the Bible. The New Science can stand on its own. I can handle the physicists."

"You know, some people are coming just to see if you'll have another seizure. They want to see how you hold up under pressure. Some want to see you fall. You're OK, right?"

"I'm all right, Jimmy. Thanks for asking. But you're always asking me that." Tobias chuckled. "I hope I disappoint them—by staying healthy and on my feet."

They smiled and continued on.

—

The theater was grand and full of history—carpeted and curtained in Oriental designs, evoking the elegance of the 1930s and '40s. The lights dimmed before Tobias's entrance. At stage left sat a semicircle of eight chairs, occupied by male and female representatives of physics and cosmology. A podium stood at center stage.

Tobias entered from stage right and stood at the podium.

"Distinguished guests and friends," he began, "you've asked to meet with me to clarify the meaning of the New Science. Some of you may find my approach disturbing—it challenges the very fiber of what you've been taught.

"I know your fields—cosmology, physics, biology— have distinct ideas about the origins of existence. The New Science offers another.

"It teaches that our universe—as far as the eye can see—is a tiny particle within an electron of a carbon atom. It may sound far-fetched, but I believe this atom exists within the brain of a living creature—probably intelligent—that lives in a larger outer universe.

"This would explain the universal intelligence we observe in everyday life. Life in our universe reflects the characteristics of the atom from which it comes."

Tobias could already hear the grumbling from the audience and the panel. He continued speaking—no notes, no hesitation—ignoring the murmurs.

"Let's say our universe is just an electron within a carbon atom in the brain of an extraterrestrial being. That being may exist within another carbon atom in a larger universe, which itself may be an electron in yet another universe—and so on. To call this being 'extraterrestrial' is inaccurate. He doesn't live on another planet. He lives in another universe. He is, more precisely, an extra-universe person—able to interact with ours."

He paused, scanning the room.

"This creates an unseen web of interactions. Our universe serves as his electron. These interactions form a vast matrix of dimensions. You are part of a universe that is an electron in the brain of a being in another universe. That being may, in turn, be part of a universe that is an electron in yet another being."

A cosmologist on the panel interrupted. "So you're saying our universe is an electron in another universe, which itself may be an electron in another? Are you reducing all of creation to a chemical reaction? Where is the Creator in all this?"

"All of this is the Creator," Tobias said, his voice reverent.

"And universes and electrons are one and the same?"

"Yes," Tobias replied. "This concept creates an interconnected matrix that reflects the true nature of the Greater Universe. And it's a two-way street. Just as our universe may be an electron in another being's brain, the electrons in our own brains may house entire universes—worlds, solar systems, galaxies. You and I may carry countless universes within us. What we do affects them. That's karma."

"So we think too small?" the cosmologist asked.

"Exactly. The infinite and the infinitesimal are one and the same," Tobias said, channeling the teachings of Stokes. "We struggle to grasp the endless nature of endlessness. Multiply the number of universes within our own by the number of carbon atoms in every living being, plant, and inanimate object—on Earth and beyond. The number is literally countless."

A thin man on the panel, his hair wispy and gray, leaned forward. "I'm a physicist. What do you base this on—other than your bump on the head?"

Laughter rippled through the panel and audience. Tobias remained calm.

"To understand our universe, let's start with our galaxy. Evidence suggests a black hole at the center of the

Milky Way. Black holes—collapsed stars—are so dense that not even light escapes. They may exist at the center of other galaxies, even at the center of our universe.

"If that's true, our universe may be a subatomic particle—an electron—on the other side of that black hole. Crossing it would place us in a larger, Greater Universe. From that vantage point, our universe would appear infinitesimal."

"What are you saying?" the physicist asked.

"The closer we get to the black hole, the closer we get to entering the surrounding universe. We're describing two interacting universes—one as electron, the other as host. If you thought we were tiny before, imagine our entire universe as an electron orbiting a carbon atom in the brain of a being in another universe."

The audience fell silent.

"This creates a matrix we've never fully considered," Tobias continued. "A fifth dimension—beyond length, width, breadth, and time. This fifth dimension is the web of connections between universes and electrons. It's not parallel universes—it's intimate intersections. Our universe is someone's electron. Our electrons may be someone else's universe."

"I see," said the physicist. "We're interacting with other universes, all serving as electrons and universes simultaneously."

"Correct. This fifth dimension is not parallel—it's relational. We exist in an intimate, interactive way."

The silence was deafening. The audience stared in disbelief. Then came the explosion—applause and jeers, awe and outrage. Tobias had just told them their vast universe was smaller than a pea—and that the pea was as vast as the universe.

"Surely, Mr. Sinclair, you intend to publish your proof," said the physicist.

Tobias smiled. "I don't need to publish it. I can demonstrate it now."

He turned to the audience.

"Every interaction in the universe involves one process: the net energy of the interaction, E. This applies to atoms, molecules, electromagnetic radiation, people, animals, inanimate objects—everything. Whether it's a chemical reaction, a conversation, or a nuclear explosion, E is the result of two interacting entities.

"If $E = mc^2$, and $c = \lambda f$, then $E = m \times (\lambda f)^2$. Frequency and wavelength travel at the speed of light. The variables are how high or low the frequencies are, and how long or short the wavelengths. This governs electromagnetic and chemical interactions—and the interactions of subatomic particles with the universe.

"For example, subtle interactions between carbon atoms and the universe may form life—a living phase of carbon. Our universe, as an electron in a carbon atom in another universe, interacts with carbon atoms here to manifest the nuanced energy we call life."

"So life itself is due to the interaction of the universe with certain forms of carbon?" asked another physicist.

"Indeed," Tobias said. "And similar interactions occur with thought and behavior. Human thoughts and actions create karma. All interactions—chemical, electromagnetic, behavioral—are E. They result from intersecting waves of matter, energy, or both.

"Your frequencies and wavelengths interact with your neighbor's, producing the total energy of your relationship. These equations have implications for physics, chemistry, biology, and behavior. Observation is the key. This is the best mathematical proof I can offer—though I am not a physicist."

"Indeed, you're not."

"Well," retorted Tobias, unable to contain himself, "can you prove that I'm wrong? It's remarkable how often opinions are shaped by bias rather than by objective observation or reasoned analysis."

The audience grumbled, breaking into a wave of irritation and misplaced relief.

"You can't have it both ways, Sinclair!" someone shouted from the mezzanine. "You claim to be a jack-of-all-trades, but you're clearly a master of none!"

"Yeah!" yelled a woman. "You're a fake!"

"You're a fraud!" shouted a man in a dark suit. "What do you know about physics?"

A young man near the rear stood up and addressed the heckler. "Hey, man, don't disrespect Mr. Sinclair. The New Science changed my life."

"Oh really?" the man sneered. "How?"

"With the New Science, I can make sense of the world—and my life. I struggled with addiction and crime. I stopped when I found God, and the New Science helped me understand why I did what I did. I've been clean for fifteen months. Tell them, Mr. Sinclair. Tell them how the New Science helps people."

Tobias hadn't anticipated this fervor. He paused, then spoke directly to the young man.

"I'm glad the New Science helped you. Its insights can have far-reaching effects. People can apply it to everyday situations, or use it to solve specific problems. When we understand the motives behind our behavior, we can adjust that behavior—and change our destiny.

"The New Science teaches that humans are capable of experiencing the true joys of the universe. When someone says they've found God—regardless of religion—they're touching the essence of the universe. They're connecting with their innate sense of right and wrong, and with the creative foundation of existence. We know when something feels right. We know when it's wrong. The universe tells us. This is the same insight described as nirvana, self-realization, the Holy Spirit, and other spiritual awakenings."

A woman on the panel interjected. "Mr. Sinclair, you started with physics and ended up at religion. I'm confused."

"That's because physics and religion are as intimately connected as the physical and the spiritual," Tobias replied. "Einstein showed us that matter and energy are one. The young man said he was blind, but now he sees. He was paralyzed, but now he moves. His physical presence is now aligned with his spiritual energy."

"With all due respect," she said, nodding toward the young man, "that's fine for him. But how does this apply to the rest of us?"

"We're like those with locked-in syndrome," Tobias said. "Not paralyzed by inability to move, but by inability to see beyond space and time. If we saw each other as beings of energy—persistent and immortal—rather than as mortal, impermanent bodies, we'd begin to grasp reality. The physical world is a reflection, a lower energy state. Our bodies are forums for spiritual interaction. Everyone is here for a reason. Everyone has a purpose."

"Yes, we know," said an older man on the panel. "The earth is a school. We've heard this before."

"Yes, I've said similar things in my New Age books," Tobias admitted. "But now it's different. The New Science offers a concrete viewpoint: our essence is spirit energy. We use our physical lives to enhance that energy. If heaven is the Greater Universe I described, then we all have everlasting life—because energy travels at light speed and cannot be destroyed. Our spirit energy enters that universe when our physical life ends. Reincarnation becomes a logical consequence. Our spirit may choose its next body. The true person is not the body, but the energy within."

Tobias motioned toward the young man. "He described how the New Science helped him use his energy wisely. It teaches us to increase positive, loving energies—and minimize fear, hate, deceit, and violence. That uplifts individuals, our species, and the planet."

The theater rumbled with applause. Others jeered and booed. Tobias raised his hand to settle the crowd. He was tempted to speak of failed civilizations and extraterrestrial aid—but whispered to himself, "Baby steps. Baby steps."

He continued. "Since we humans can understand the concept of God, harming another human is a form of harming God. We are made in God's image. To mistreat each other is to mistreat God.

"Killing animals or plants for food is part of nature's design. But even farming must honor nature and God—avoid overfishing, dispose of waste properly, avoid cruelty. But to harm a being capable of conceptualizing God is wrong. To kill each other is to destroy an aspect of God. If we continue this way, we are not ready to evolve. We are a doomed species."

Tobias looked at the panel, then at the audience.

"I am only the messenger. You must decide what to believe."

A long silence followed. Then the elderly physicist asked, "Mr. Sinclair, what are you suggesting we do?"

"Forgive one another. Let's designate today as the Day of Forgiveness. We can't wait. If we want to use the New Science to help humanity, we must first purify our minds and our species.

"If you've had conflict with anyone—if a past wrong still lingers—now is the time to forgive. Even without an apology. Forgive yourselves. Forgive your family, your friends, your enemies. Let groups forgive other groups. Let countries forgive countries. Let religions, sects, and all man-made divisions forgive one another.

"If we universally embrace love and forgiveness, we will finally be on the path to survival."

Tobias felt light-headed. He recognized the signs. A seizure was near.

"I'll leave you tonight with much food for thought," he said. "Love and forgive one another. Good night."

The eight panelists stood almost in unison—some smiling, others grim—and walked offstage. The audience, with only light applause, began to file out. Tobias stood alone at the podium, gripping it as if it were the only thing keeping him upright.

Jimmy approached from offstage. "Are you all right?"

Tobias nodded, trying to clear his head. "There you go again."

"Well," Jimmy said, "at least you didn't mention the Bible."

"I think I mentioned everything but the Bible," Tobias replied. "They'll need time to digest it all."

They walked together offstage, Jimmy acutely aware of Tobias's vulnerable state. As they exited through a side door, Jimmy said, "I don't know if I could digest it all either, TS. You tied quantum physics, God, evolution—and I don't even know what else—into one talk. You even mentioned a person in another universe. TS, you've got me worried. What's going on?"

"I don't know, Jimmy," Tobias replied. He paused to greet a few admirers and sign books before leaving the theater. The Manhattan streets were subdued, but the cool night air felt refreshing.

As they walked west toward Jimmy's car, a figure approached from the opposite direction.

"Hey, TS," Jimmy said. "Isn't that Professor Stokes?"

Tobias sighed. "Yes. That's him." He hesitated. "Jimmy, I never told you—I had a second meeting with Stokes last year."

"Why didn't you tell me?"

"I didn't want you to worry. And I didn't want you to think I'd lost my mind. Jimmy, everything Stokes said about being from an extraterrestrial community—it's true."

"What? How do you know?"

"I was on a spaceship. I'll explain later."

Jimmy stared at Tobias as Stokes reached them.

"Good evening, gentlemen," Stokes said. "Mr. Sinclair, your presentation tonight was brilliant—but we must talk."

"Hello, Mr. Stokes," Tobias replied. "Thank you. This is my assistant, Jimmy Rudolph. We can speak freely in front of him."

Jimmy nodded but remained silent.

"Mr. Sinclair, I'll be blunt. You're revealing too much. In the wrong hands, this knowledge could accelerate humanity's destruction. Your Day of Forgiveness is noble, but your discussion of the fifth-dimensional matrix could be catastrophic. My community had to make an abrupt decision."

"Yes?"

"Though we avoid interfering with intelligent species, we warned you that your accidental knowledge could be dangerous. We've worked for millennia to prevent this outcome. We left the choice to you—but now we must insist. For your protection, and humanity's, you must come with us."

"Come where?"

"Back to the ship. Your knowledge has become a liability."

Jimmy stepped forward. "Listen, Professor—Mr. Sinclair isn't going anywhere until you explain yourself."

"Jimmy," Tobias said gently, "you don't know all the facts. That's my fault. I should've told you sooner. Stokes took me to a spacecraft last year. I met extraterrestrials, hybrids, and others."

"And where was the hidden camera?" Jimmy asked, half-joking.

Stokes interjected, "We expected skepticism. Mr. Rudolph, your reaction confirms our fears. If even you—so closely tied to the New Science—can't accept our existence, what hope is there for humanity's understanding?"

Jimmy looked down, then turned to Tobias. "Do you believe him, TS?"

Tobias met his gaze. "I've seen it with my own eyes. They showed me footage—Sphinx, pyramids, Machu Picchu, Easter Island—being built thousands of years ago."

"This is why we urge you to come," Stokes continued. "We've monitored human transmissions. Based on our observations—what you'd call eavesdropping—you're in grave danger. Many people feel the New Science threatens their professions, even though you haven't contradicted their teachings."

"I've only asked them to see things from a different perspective," Tobias said.

"Yes," Stokes nodded. "But most traditionalists don't see nuance. They see challenge. They see disruption. And they don't like it. They see you as a threat."

"A threat to what?"

"To their philosophy. Their way of life," Stokes replied. "When people feel threatened, they don't seek understanding—they seek elimination. Mr. Sinclair, our data shows that many want to silence you. Others want to elevate you into a New Age guru."

"Guru?"

"We advise you to resist both extremes. Promote the New Science from afar. Write. Broadcast. Stay alive and productive. But for safety, you must come with us."

Jimmy and Tobias exchanged a look, then turned back to Stokes.

"You already know about those who want to harm you," Stokes said. "And you know some believe you're the Antichrist."

"The Antichrist?" Jimmy exclaimed.

"Well, I guess I'm in good company," Tobias said, unfazed. "Plenty of presidents have been called that."

"Yes," Stokes replied. "But they had Secret Service protection. You don't. And the group of greatest concern is a Christian sect that emerged from your teachings. They're serious—and growing fast."

Jimmy, now listening intently, asked, "Who are they?"

"They call themselves the Children of the Light," Stokes said. "They base their beliefs on the first four books of the New Testament—and on your teachings since the mugging."

"OK," Tobias said. "So they like my writings. They're religious. How does that affect me?"

"They believe you broke the code," Stokes explained. "They believe you've brought humanity full circle."

He pulled a thin pamphlet from his pocket and read aloud:

'Jesus said in the Book of John, "Moses
himself had spoken of me." Tobias   Sinclair, in turn, may
also say, "Jesus spoke of me as the Helper who would come
during the End Times." In John 15:26 it is written, "The
Helper will come—the Spirit, who   reveals the truth
about God and who comes from the Father," Jesus said. "I
will send him to you from the Father, and he will speak
about me." Tobias, the Helper, is just an   ordinary man,
*   just as Jesus was a carpenter. His task is to help*
inform humankind of its   true nature and of the full
nature of the universe. The Second Coming of Jesus was
*   fulfilled by the development of the full*
understanding of the meaning of Christ's ministry,   which
is really the teaching of what it means to be human. Out of
Judaism came Christ, and out of Christianity came Tobias.'

"This group began after your first meeting with the
theologians," Stokes said. "When you announced—during
a seizure—that you were the Helper from the New
Testament."

"I only vaguely remember that," Tobias said, puzzled.

Jimmy nodded. "You were having a seizure at the
time."

Stokes continued, "Seizure or not, those who were
listening didn't forget what you said. They've formed a
growing movement—determined to observe you as a
biblical figure, the Helper of the New Age. This group has
grown exponentially since we last met, Mr. Sinclair."

Tobias stared at Stokes, subtly bracing himself against
a parked car as he felt light-headed. Jimmy grabbed his arm

211

at the elbow and whispered, "TS, what's happening? Is another seizure coming on?"

"No. I'll be OK," Tobias whispered, steadying himself as his head cleared.

Jimmy asked, "Can I see that tract, Mr. Stokes?" He examined the pamphlet, then looked at Tobias. "This group tried to contact the school. Mill and I dismissed them as just another fringe group. We didn't take them seriously."

"On the contrary," Stokes said. "They're very serious. They even have a plot to kidnap Mr. Sinclair and force him to become their leader."

Tobias, regaining focus, said, "Didn't you mention something like this during our drive upstate last year?"

"Yes. But the groups have grown larger—and more powerful. They're gaining political and religious influence. Society is shifting. Communications we've monitored show a growing divide: those who believe in the New Science, and those who don't. And both sides are drawing lines."

"You mean battle lines," Jimmy said, handing the pamphlet back.

Tobias shook his head. "The New Science is supposed to unite people—not tear them apart."

"The bottom line is that you must not be around," said Stokes. "Otherwise, you really won't be around."

Jimmy narrowed his eyes. "That sounds like a threat."

"It's a statement of fact. You have nothing to fear from me, my friend. But the choice is yours. I urge you to contact me soon."

Stokes walked past them and disappeared around the corner. Tobias was shaken as they continued toward Jimmy's car.

Driving back to Brooklyn, Jimmy broke the silence. "Never trust anyone who calls you 'my friend,'" he said, sounding older than his years.

"It's funny," Tobias replied. "In a strange way, Stokes and I really are friends. But I feel edgier now than I did when I met the extraterrestrials."

"TS, I've got to be honest—I still find it hard to believe you boarded a spaceship and met aliens. I'm not calling you a liar, but are you sure it wasn't a seizure?"

Tobias's voice sharpened. "No, Jimmy. It wasn't a seizure. You wouldn't believe what I saw. And yet, it all made sense. The ancient stone sites—they're relics from a past age. And now, I see the real problem."

"What problem?"

"The human being," Tobias said. "It's in our nature to fight and destroy ourselves—civilization after civilization. Our aggressive nature is the root."

"So what can we do?"

"Educate ourselves about the true nature of the universe. If we did, violence would seem primitive.

Bombing each other would feel barbaric. Knowledge is the only way to break the cycle."

As they crossed the Brooklyn Bridge, Jimmy nodded. "I guess that's what Stokes meant—stay alive so you can keep teaching."

"But he said I can't stay on Earth. And I can't tell anyone why I'm leaving."

"Why not?"

"For the same reasons I didn't tell you. I don't want to cause panic—or be labeled insane. Besides, revealing the truth would blow Stokes's cover. His community abandoned humanity long ago to let us evolve. They still believe we're not ready for a sudden introduction. They won't land on the White House lawn. But Stokes said they plan a 'Great Landing'—when the time is right. They won't hand us the New Science. We have to earn it."

"So what are you going to do, TS?"

Tobias paused. "I'm going with Stokes. Only you and Mill will know where I am. I can't even tell my family. We'll say I prefer to write and speak from an undisclosed location."

"An undisclosed location? In outer space?"

"Jimmy, I need to share what I've learned since the mugging. People don't need to know where I am. If the New Science can help save humanity, do I really have a choice?"

They rode in silence. When Jimmy pulled up to Tobias's building, Tobias opened the door and placed one foot on the curb.

"Thanks," he said. "Keep in touch. Things are going to move fast."

Jimmy waited until Tobias was safely inside before driving off.

Tobias entered his apartment and turned on the lights. He sat on the edge of his bed, scanning the room. It felt starker than ever—emptier, as if it knew its days with him were numbered.

He realized he'd painted himself into a corner. Even if he left with Stokes, he might not be missed. His pursuit of enlightenment had distanced him from nearly everyone. He had paid a high price in service to others. And now, he felt he had lost his way.

The lives of his family and friends would go on—without him.

Struck by the thought, he began to cry. He felt he had failed. He couldn't see a way out.

The phone rang. It was Mill.

Tobias wiped his face and cleared his throat before answering.

"How did it go tonight?" she asked.

"Mill, I need to see you. Something's happened."

"What is it?"

"I was at the theater with Jimmy. We ran into Stokes. I need to fill you in."

"I'll be right over."

Mill hadn't attended the program—she preferred working behind the scenes. Even as Tobias had distanced himself, she had remained devoted to the New Science University. Her role had become her calling. It was a marriage of purpose and fulfillment—a two-way street. And she had found peace in it.

It was a short walk from Mill's apartment to Tobias's building, but it felt like an eternity as he waited for her to ring the bell.

While he waited, Tobias called his family in Philadelphia. He spoke with his mother and son. His sister was away.

He tried to sound normal, but he knew this might be the last time he'd speak to them for a long while.

His son sensed something.

"Pop, I know that tone in your voice. What's up?"

"I guess I have to be on my toes around you."

"Are you working on another book or project that'll keep you away again?"

"Yeah. Something like that."

"Don't you think I understand by now? I understand you. And you understand me—"

Tobias interrupted. "David, I've got something to tell you."

"Yes?"

"I need to leave New York."

"Are you coming back to Philadelphia?"

"No. I can't tell you where I'm going, but I'll be away for quite a while."

There was a long silence as David tried to absorb what his father was saying.

"Dad," he said somberly, "I thought we were finally getting close. I thought we could be a family again. Why are you leaving us?"

"It's hard to explain, David," Tobias said, realizing he didn't fully understand it himself. "But I'm not leaving you. You'll always be close to my heart. I have a mission to accomplish—and I can't do it by staying in New York."

David's voice trembled with restrained anger. "Pop, you always choose your work over your family. When will it be our turn?"

"I didn't expect you to understand right away. But I'm doing this to help our family—and families everywhere."

"There you go again, Pop," David said. "Grandma says you always talk with your head in the clouds."

"Show some respect, boy. I'm still your father!" Tobias snapped, unprepared for the sting of David's words.

A heavy silence followed. Both regrouped, softening their tones.

"Dad," David said quietly, "I need you in my life."

"I will be," Tobias replied, fighting back a tear. "I'll keep in touch every chance I get. We'll keep the channels open."

"You got it, Pop," David said, trying to mask his disappointment—long accustomed to his father's fleeting farewells.

"Tell Grandma and Aunt Janice I love them."

"We love you, too."

The phone clicked off just as Mill rang the doorbell. Tobias let her in.

"Change of plans," he said abruptly.

"I'm ready for anything. Spill it," she said, settling onto the familiar couch.

"Tonight I told Jimmy something I've kept to myself for a long time. You should know it too. In fact, you and Jimmy will be the only ones to know." Tobias looked directly at her. "Everything I said about Stokes was real. I saw it for myself. He took me aboard a spaceship—with humans, extraterrestrials, and hybrids."

Mill didn't flinch. "Go on."

"Stokes believes I'm in danger from people who don't understand the New Science. He said I should stay with them—for protection. I can teach from afar."

"Where will you go?"

"Aboard a spaceship. Maybe it'll just hover around Earth. Honestly, I don't know."

"And you're willing to go with Stokes and people from outer space?"

"He said it's my choice," Tobias replied. "And I'm choosing for you and Jimmy to be my contacts on Earth. I'll teach and write from an undisclosed location. You're already running the business side of the school anyway."

"You'd better believe it, Toby!"

"Mill, aren't you shocked by any of this?"

"Toby," she said, "at this stage of the game, nothing—absolutely nothing—surprises me about you."

"One last thing," Tobias said. "I'm calling Stokes tomorrow. I need to go soon—before I change my mind. I want you and Jimmy to see me off."

"See you off?"

"I want you both to witness the spacecraft's departure. Otherwise, it'll feel too much like abduction—even though I'm going willingly."

"OK, Toby. Just let me know when and where. Are you sure about this?"

"I'm not sure about anything, Mill. I'm putting my trust in Stokes—and all my eggs in one basket."

"Why?"

"To help humanity break the cycle of self-destruction. The New Science must be taught by one of our own. I don't care if it's me. This work must be done."

"OK, my dear. I know you know what you're doing."

"Well, that makes one of us."

They shared a laugh—something they hadn't done in months. Then, almost telepathically, they realized they might not see each other again for a long time. They stood, eyes welling, and embraced—perhaps for the first time in decades. Loose ends tied, Tobias felt ready for tomorrow.

"Let me know if you need anything," Mill said as she left the apartment.

Tobias remained alone with his thoughts. He thought of his family in Philadelphia, his chosen family in New York, and the uncertain future ahead. He fell asleep on the sofa, exhausted.

———

The next morning was cloudy and wet. Tobias wondered if the weather would affect his flight—then remembered extraterrestrial technology didn't follow human rules.

He contacted Stokes, who agreed to let Jimmy and Mill witness the departure.

By midday, the three were in Stokes's car, heading to upstate New York. Jimmy's car was in the shop, and he and Mill planned to take a bus back. The ride was quiet, filled only with small talk and roadside curiosities.

By the time they reached the isolated destination near the Canadian border, the sun had set. Stars pierced the twilight.

Stokes turned down a private road on an old farm. In a clearing, the spacecraft hovered above the young trees. Jimmy and Mill, sitting in the backseat, were mesmerized. Tobias and Stokes, veterans now, barely reacted.

Stokes stopped at the edge of the clearing. The ship glowed silently.

He turned to Jimmy. "Young man, you may have this car. I have no further need of it." He signed over the title and registration.

"Thank you, Mr. Stokes," Jimmy said. "This ride sure beats my jalopy."

Tobias remained withdrawn but resolute. The four stepped out and stood beside the car. The ship floated silently before them. The familiar door opened, releasing the stairway.

Tobias hugged Jimmy and Mill.

He handed Jimmy his apartment keys. "The rent's paid through the year. You and Yolanda need more space for Grace. You'll finally turn my bare apartment into a real home."

Jimmy's eyes glistened. "I don't know what to say, TS."

"This way, you won't have to travel so far to work with Mill."

Mill shrugged. "Sorry, kid. I've got nothing to give you!"

They shared one final laugh and embraced in a group hug.

Stokes waited near the ramp. "Mr. Sinclair, it is time."

Tobias walked toward the ship, paused at the steps, and gave a final wave. He entered the craft, followed by Stokes. The stairway retracted. The door slid shut.

The spacecraft rose silently above the car. Jimmy and Mill watched as it accelerated into the deep-indigo night. As the spacecraft vanished, Tobias Sinclair left behind the world he had known—not in retreat, but in quiet defiance of history's cycles. He had chosen the unknown, not for glory, but for the hope that humanity might finally learn to forgive, to evolve, and to endure. He left behind the noise of Earth for the silence between stars, carrying with him the fragile hope that love, reason, and forgiveness might yet rewrite the fate of a species. The sky did not close; it opened. The stars did not blink; they watched. Where thought bends and time breathes, the New Science had only just begun to echo. And somewhere in the folds of time, a new myth was being written.

About the Author

From an early age, Paul Anthony Corley has been drawn to the world's enduring mysteries — ancient structures, cryptic writings, and the myths that shape our understanding of reality. As both a physician and a science fiction author, he explores the intersection of logic and wonder, offering bold interpretations of seemingly illogical phenomena.

Writing under the name P.A. Corley in his medical publications, and Paul Anthony in his fiction, he bridges disciplines to challenge long-held beliefs and illuminate new possibilities. His work often complements conventional wisdom while quietly subverting it — inviting readers to question, reflect, and reimagine.

In his novel, *Day of Forgiveness*, and its sequel, *An Abundance of Caution*, Paul blends emotional depth with philosophical inquiry, crafting a story that explores forgiveness, alien contact, and the fragile bonds of family. His ultimate goal is to make the human experience more insightful — one revelation at a time.

Call to Action

If this book moved you, challenged you, or inspired reflection, please consider leaving a review on Amazon. Your feedback helps others discover the journey—and supports the ongoing mission of *Day of Forgiveness.*

An Abundance of Caution – the exciting sequel

Tobias Sinclair's journey continues beyond the indigo night. As he ventures deeper into the galaxy, he faces new challenges—not only from alien civilizations, but from the lingering shadows of Earth's past. In this direct continuation of *Day of Forgiveness*, Tobias must confront the limits of reason, the cost of leadership, and the fragile hope of universal peace.

Visit https://www.An-Abundance-of-Caution.com. Watch the videos, read the sequel, and join the adventure!